CAKE AND CRIMINALS

KATHLEEN SUZETTE

❀ Created with Vellum

SIGN UP

Sign up to receive my newsletter for updates on new releases and sales:

https://www.subscribepage.com/kathleen-suzette

Follow me on Facebook:

https://www.facebook.com/Kathleen-Suzette-Kate-Bell-authors-759206390932120

CHAPTER 1

"You're killing me with the suspense."

Alec looked up at me, one eyebrow raised, his black hair shining beneath the light that hung over our table. "What are you talking about? How long have you been married to me? Don't you know this is how it goes? You say you want to do something, and I think about it for a while. A long while." He grinned.

I rolled my eyes. "Let's go on a vacation this year. We never get to go anywhere." Alec was a detective with the local police force, and it seemed like something always got in the way, preventing us from taking time to just enjoy ourselves.

He took a sip of his iced tea and set the glass back

on the table. "All right then, we'll take a vacation. How does next month sound? I'll put in the request tomorrow."

I nodded. "That sounds great. Where are we going to go? Don't tell me you don't have any ideas, because I don't believe you."

He shrugged. "I don't have any place in mind. Honestly, as long as I get to spend time with you, that's the only thing that's important to me."

I smiled. "Aren't you the most wonderful husband in the whole world? I only want to spend time with you, too. Let's go someplace fun. What about Hawaii? Or Italy? We love Italian food. We should go to Italy." I could just picture us taking a ride on a gondola while a man sang to us in Italian. My long, curly red hair would fan out over my shoulders as I rested my head on Alec's shoulder. How much more romantic could you get?

His eyes widened. "Italy? That sounds expensive. I thought you wanted to go to the beach or someplace not quite so exotic."

I sighed. "I'm sure Italy is expensive. But we've never gone any place like that together, and I think it would be a lot of fun. Don't you want to try out authentic Italian food?"

"I thought Antonio's was authentic Italian food?" he asked with a wink.

I turned back to my lobster roll. "Sure, I suppose it's authentic, but I bet it's not authentic-authentic. You know?" I grabbed the lobster roll and took a bite, almost groaning at the delicious, slightly sweet flavor of the lobster meat and the fluffy softness of the roll. Stan's Crab Shack had the best lobster rolls in all of Maine. The roll was soft and buttery and yummy.

He chuckled and took a bite of a crab cake and nodded appreciatively. "This is so good. Why don't we come here more often? It takes less than ten minutes to get here, and the service is great, not to mention the food is delicious. We should be eating here every night."

I chuckled. "We could do that if you really wanted to. But on second thought, all the money we would save by not coming here every night would easily pay for a trip to Italy within a year. I bet it would be a lot less than a year." I took another bite of my lobster roll. Stan's was reasonably priced, but like everything these days, prices have gone up.

"How about we focus on vacationing someplace closer?"

I looked at him with one eyebrow raised. "Closer?

How much closer? Don't say the beach." As much as I loved the beach, I wanted to go someplace else.

He shrugged. "What about Chebeague Island? I bet there's someplace nice to stay there. We could spend a weekend just relaxing."

I almost groaned. "Chebeague Island? I was hoping for something a little more exotic."

"We could go to Alabama to see your mother?"

I sighed. "Yeah, I guess we could. Not that Alabama is exotic." My mother came to Maine frequently to visit, especially with the birth of her first great-grandbaby and my first grandbaby a year and a half earlier. As much as I loved Goose Bay, the small town where I had grown up, I wanted to go someplace else.

He smiled. "How about we save up for a delightful trip to Italy and choose something a little less expensive for this summer? If you want to go to Hawaii, we'll do it. You decide."

I took a sip of my iced tea, thinking this over. Hawaii would be fun, but it would be expensive, too. If we were going to save up for a trip to Italy, then we probably needed to do something less expensive this summer. "Let me think about it."

I looked up and spotted Lori Lynch walking

through the door of the crab shack. She was wearing a pair of white jeans and a floral top that showed her cleavage. She stopped at the deserted hostess station and glanced around. When she spotted me, we made eye contact, and she smiled and hurried over.

"Oh Allie, I'm so glad I ran into you here." She glanced at Alec. "Good evening, Alec. Good to see you, too."

Alec nodded. "How are you doing, Lori?"

She smiled without answering him and turned back to me. "Allie, I've been thinking about you. This weekend is the annual fundraiser for the animal rescue. What do you say to making a nice lemon pound cake for the silent auction?"

I sat up. "Oh gosh, is the fundraiser this weekend? How could I forget? I would love to make a lemon pound cake. I love that this fundraiser is held every year to help the poor animals." Lori was in her mid-forties with white-blond hair, and her nails were stylishly manicured. She ran the Fluffs and Stuffs Rescue like a well-oiled machine.

She nodded, and I caught a whiff of heavy perfume. "You know I live for those animals. I would do anything to make sure they're all taken care of, as well as spayed and neutered. We're having a spaghetti dinner, as you know, as well as the dessert auction afterward."

I nodded. "I haven't attended the fundraiser for a couple of years, but we should do that, Alec. Doesn't it sound like fun?" I turned to him.

He nodded. "Sure, I like spaghetti as much as the next person. We should go."

I turned back to Lori. "I need to buy some tickets then. Where do I get those?"

She grinned. "You can get them from me, but I don't have any on me now. If you call the shelter, we can take care of it. I appreciate that you're going to donate a cake."

I nodded. "I would be more than happy to make a cake. I could also make some cupcakes, and maybe even a pie, too. This will be so much fun."

She shook her head. "Oh no, that's fine. I just need one cake. If you make a lemon cake pound cake, I will be eternally grateful."

"Oh, it's no trouble to make some cupcakes and a pie to go along with the cake. It doesn't take me long to make them, and I don't mind at all."

She smiled. "Like I said, Allie, I would be thrilled if you would make a lemon pound cake for the auction. But that's really all I need."

I was surprised that she was turning down my offer of cupcakes and a pie, too. Didn't she want to make money for the rescue? "I can make a lovely lemon cake with a lemon buttercream frosting. I have a fantastic recipe, and I love lemon. I think everybody loves lemon, don't you?"

She nodded and sighed. "Yes, that sounds interesting, but I really just want a lemon *pound* cake from you. Do you have a recipe for lemon pound cake?"

I gazed at her, not sure what was going on. Why did she just want a plain old lemon pound cake? Why didn't she want something fancier? It would bring in more money for the rescue. "Sure, I've got a great lemon pound cake recipe that my grandmama gave me. Just think about all the money you could raise for the rescue if I made cupcakes and pies as well, though. I don't mind. I would love to make them and donate them to such a noble cause."

She smiled, but it seemed forced now. "Allie, I appreciate your enthusiasm, but I just need the lemon pound cake. You call me about those tickets tomorrow, and we'll make arrangements to have the cake picked up tomorrow. Now then, I am starving, and I have got to get something to eat. It was good running into the two of you." With that, she turned and headed back to the hostess station.

I turned to Alec. "What was that all about? Why didn't she want me to make cupcakes?"

He shrugged and took another bite of his dinner. "Maybe she's got all she needs."

I sighed and took a bite of my lobster roll. When I swallowed, I said, "I can make two dozen cupcakes, a cherry pie, and maybe a peach pie. I have always loved peach pie."

He looked at me with one eyebrow raised. "I thought Lori said she only wanted a lemon pound cake from you?"

I gazed at him and then narrowed my eyes. "That's silly. She needs to bring in as much money as she can for the animals to make sure they have a home and medical treatment. Why would she turn down the opportunity to have more baked goods to sell? It doesn't make any sense. I'll just make a few extra things, and I know she'll appreciate it once she sees them."

He chuckled, shook his head, and went back to eating his dinner.

"What are you chuckling about?"

He looked up at me. "You're not very good at following instructions."

I narrowed my eyes at him. "What are you talking about? Following instructions? I'm great at it. It doesn't matter what I do, I put my all into it."

He smiled at me. "You're not following instructions. For whatever reason, she's decided that she wants nothing more than a lemon pound cake from you, but you're determined to do your own thing and make what you want. Just follow the instructions."

I eyed him, feeling a bit irritated now. "When something doesn't make sense, sometimes you have to improvise. It doesn't make sense that she doesn't want more baked goods to sell, so I'm improvising."

He shook his head and chuckled, but didn't say anything else, and that just aggravated me more. Lori was placing an order at the counter, probably to go. Why was she turning me down for more baked goods? I shook my head. "Everybody loves cupcakes. She could sell them for at least three dollars apiece and make some extra money. If I make them a little fancier, she can sell them for four or five dollars apiece. Why would she turn down extra money for the rescue?"

"Maybe this is a test to see if you can follow directions."

I snorted. "I can follow directions just fine. I'm improvising. You should be supporting me because you know I'm more than eager to help a good cause."

Minutes later, Lori got her order, and as she was leaving the crab shack, she gave me a little wave, her fingers waggling in the air. I could make lemon cupcakes and the lemon pound cake. A wonderful buttercream frosting would top off the cupcakes, and maybe I could figure out how to put little puppies and kittens on top of each cupcake. Brilliant.

CHAPTER 2

My black cat, Dixie, rubbed against my legs as I set out the ingredients for my lemon pound cake on the kitchen counter. My grandmama had taught me to bake, and I had a lot of recipes that had been handed down from her. The lemon pound cake recipe was one of my favorites, but one I hadn't made in a long time. I gazed at the small, yellowed recipe card written in Grandmama's hand-writing, and a tear came to my eye. I grew up in Alabama, and she had lived next door to my family. I spent many summer afternoons at her house, learning how to cream butter and sugar perfectly and the importance of sifting flour. There had been so many lessons I had learned at her side, and she had filled the hours with chatter of family stories. She had been gone for over twenty years now, but it felt like yesterday when she had taught me the secrets of flaky pie crust.

I reached down and scratched Dixie's head. "If it weren't for Lori Lynch, who knows where you would be?" Dixie had been a spur-of-the-moment adoption. Fluffs and Stuffs Rescue housed a large number of cats and dogs, but usually not for long. She would get them from overfilled shelters or from people who had found them on the side of the road, and then contact other shelters across the country, transporting them herself in many instances so they could help adopt them out. I was glad we had a facility like that so sweethearts like Dixie could find a permanent, loving home. Dixie began purring as I continued petting him. He was getting older now, but he still got frisky in the early morning hours, and batted pens, cups, and other things off of countertops.

Straightening up, I washed my hands and put the rest of the ingredients out on the counter. I was sorely tempted to make those cupcakes, but what Alec had said about me not being able to follow directions returned to me. I didn't want to admit it, but several teachers had remarked the same thing to my mother when I was a little girl. Not that I didn't want to follow the rules, but I could see so many alternate ways of doing things, and I couldn't imagine why others couldn't see them too. So, I frequently took my own path to doing homework or playing games.

The doorbell rang, and I turned to get it when my daughter, Jennifer, hollered, "I got it!" from the other room.

Jennifer was home from college for the summer and was making sleeping in a habit. That was fine. It wouldn't be long before she would have to face reality and find a job when she graduated.

A few moments later, Jennifer and my best friend, Lucy Gray, entered the kitchen.

"Good morning," I said to Lucy.

She smiled. "Good morning, Allie. So, what have you got going on today? You're baking a cake, right? What about cupcakes? Pies?" she asked, pulling up a stool to the kitchen island. "I'm here to help."

Jennifer went to the coffee pot. "Coffee, Lucy?"

"I would love a cup of coffee," she said.

I went to the refrigerator, got the creamer out, and brought it to the kitchen island. "Lori Lynch says all she wants from me is a lemon pound cake." I put my hands on my hips and gazed at her as I let that sink in.

Her brow furrowed. "Lemon pound cake? As in, *one* lemon pound cake?"

I nodded. "One. Just one."

She shook her head slowly. "How are you going to pull that off? I don't think you've ever baked just one of anything in your entire life."

Jennifer snorted. "If Mom is doing the baking, we're going to get a lot of baked goods, whatever it is." She brought over two cups of coffee and set one in front of Lucy. "You should be excited about just baking one pound cake. It won't take you any time at all."

I ignored her. "I offered to make cupcakes and pies too, but she said no. Why? Doesn't she want to earn a lot of money for the shelter? Isn't that what this dinner is all about? It doesn't make sense." I'd been racking my brain trying to figure out why she would turn me down for more baked goods, and I couldn't come up with anything. Maybe it was a pride thing. I had a reputation in Sandy Harbor for making some of the best sweets around, and it made me happy when others enjoyed what I made. If I was only baking one lemon pound cake, then only one person would enjoy it when it was auctioned off. But even setting that aside, it still didn't make sense that she didn't want more baked goods to sell.

Lucy shook her head and poured creamer into her cup. "No, that doesn't make any sense, does it? I don't know what she's thinking. You're offering to do some baking for her charitable organization, and she's turning you down?"

I nodded and picked up my now cold cup of coffee, taking a sip. "That's what I thought. It doesn't make any sense. I told Alec I was going to make some cupcakes anyway and bring them to her, and he told me I had trouble following directions. Can you believe it?"

Jennifer laughed and snorted. "Yeah, I can believe he said that. It's true."

I rolled my eyes, giving her long red hair a playful tug. "What do you know about it?"

She pulled up a stool and sat down. "Third grade, PTA fundraiser. You were supposed to bring an apple pie, and you brought an apple pie, cinnamon rolls, chocolate chip cookies, and three cakes. Three." She looked at me meaningfully. "All the other kids wanted to know if you worked at a bakery or something. It was embarrassing."

I shook my head. "What do you mean, it was embarrassing? Everyone loved everything I brought. You got points for being the kid who brought in the most money. If I remember right, you were then able to order some books that you got to keep for yourself." My kid. She was an introvert, and any kind of attention drawn to her was unappreciated.

She rolled her eyes. "Okay, fine. I got some books out of it, and I certainly appreciated that. But you should have followed directions and just brought the apple pie."

Lucy took a sip of her coffee. "What's Lori going to do if you bring a couple dozen cupcakes? Say no? Turn them down?"

I took another sip of my cold coffee. "Exactly. I could pipe some cute little puppies and kittens on each of the cupcakes, and I'm telling you, she could get five bucks apiece. Six, even. People will pay a little more when it's going to a good cause. Maybe she could get seven dollars for them."

Jennifer rolled her eyes yet again. "Mom, don't go crazy. Just do what she wants you to do."

I sighed. My creativity was being stifled. "Fine. *One* lemon pound cake."

"It will be the best lemon pound cake ever," Lucy said.

I nodded. "Yeah, I'm sure it will be."

Lucy turned to Jennifer. "What are you doing for the summer, Jennifer?"

She shrugged. "Just hanging out, I guess. I have a job at the movie theater on the weekends."

I turned to look at her. She had been unusually quiet since she had come home. "What's going on with you?" I asked. "You've got one more year of college. Please tell me you're going to finish up this year." Last year she had made a sudden decision and had taken the fall semester off. That meant she didn't get to graduate in May. She had also changed her major from biology to teaching, which meant having to take a few more classes as well.

She shrugged but couldn't help but smile. "Nothing is going on with me. And yes, I'm going to graduate next year. There. Are you happy?"

My youngest child was awful at keeping things from me. There was something else going on. "Why are you smiling?"

She took a sip of her coffee, smiling around the edge of the cup. "Don't you want your children to be happy?" she asked.

I narrowed my eyes. "Of course I do. Spill it," I urged.

"Don't keep secrets from us," Lucy said as Dixie came to rub up against her leg.

Jennifer laughed. "Okay, I may have met a guy. A very nice guy."

I was all ears. "What's his name? What's he like? Where did you meet him?"

"Mom, don't be so nosy," she said and poured a dash more creamer into her coffee.

I shook my head. "You're not getting off that easily. Spill it."

She was nearly bursting with happiness. "His name is Tyler Jackson, and I met him at school. In the library, to be precise. We got to talking, and he asked me out. We've been dating for three months, and I really like him."

I gasped. "Three months? And you're just now telling me about him?"

"Oh, Jennifer, I'm so happy for you," Lucy said, patting her hand.

"Thank you, Lucy," Jennifer said. "Mom, you're nosy. That's why I didn't say anything, especially after, well, you know."

I knew. We had thought that her last boyfriend

was going to be a permanent fixture in our lives, but they had broken up last year, and she had been devastated by it. It was nice to see her happy again. "I'm excited for you, Jennifer," I said. "And I would love to meet him. I promise to try not to be nosy, but you know I probably will be."

She laughed. "I kind of figured as much. Maybe I'll bring him around to meet you sometime soon."

"What is he studying in school?" Lucy asked.

"He studied to be a nurse," she said. "He graduated in May and is looking for a job now."

I nodded. "That sounds fantastic. I would love to meet him. Has he lived here in Maine all his life?"

"And does his family live here?" Lucy asked.

She nodded. "Yes, he was born here in Maine and has lived here all his life. His family lives here, too. I'd better get upstairs and get dressed because we're going out to lunch today."

"Oh, I can meet him when he comes to pick you up," I said, turning to Lucy. She nodded, grinning.

"No, sorry, but I'm going to pick him up. His car is in the shop today. I'll talk to the two of you later." She turned and left the kitchen, padding up the stairs to her room.

I turned to Lucy. "She looks happy."

She nodded. "She looks very happy. And I'm happy for her. It will be nice for her to have someone who cares for her and will be an important part of her life."

I nodded and got the flour canister from the counter. When your children are healthy and happy, that's really all that matters in life.

CHAPTER 3

"That looks delicious," Lucy said, peering over the lemon pound cake. I had just finished pouring a thin layer of lemon icing on top of it.

"Thank you. I love anything lemon, and this cake has my mouth watering," I replied. After baking the lemon pound cake and allowing it to cool, I made some candied lemon slices, breaking one end of each slice and twisting it before laying it on top. It was perfect, if I did say so myself.

"I'm glad you made a couple of small ones on the side," Lucy said. "You know how Ed loves your lemon pound cake. For that matter, Ed loves everything you make."

I chuckled. "There's nothing like having the full support of your friends in every endeavor." If you're ever lacking friends, I heartily recommend learning how to bake. They'll be coming out of the woodwork.

She grabbed a wet washcloth and began cleaning up the counter for me. "You know you can count on me and Ed."

I nodded, gazing at the cake. I had purchased a lovely green glass cake stand I was donating along with the cake. Maybe it would help to increase the bids on it. The doorbell rang, and I glanced at Lucy. "I wonder who that could be?" I took my apron off, tossed it on a chair, and headed to the front door. Jennifer had left earlier, and Alec was at work. I still hadn't made anything for dinner yet and I needed to figure something out, I thought as I headed to the door. When I opened it, I was surprised to see Lori Lynch standing there.

"Good afternoon, Allie. I brought the tickets you wanted for the dinner tomorrow night, and I thought I would pick up the cake if it's ready," she said with a smile.

I hadn't expected her to drop by to pick up the cake since I had told her I would bring it to her house when I finished. "Goodness, you've got great timing. I just finished with the cake. Why don't you come inside, and I'll put it into a bakery box for you." I stepped back, holding the door open for her, and she stepped into the house.

"Oh, I love what you've done with this place. It was in terrible shape when you bought it, wasn't it?"

I nodded and shut the door. "It needed quite a bit of work. There are still a few rooms that Alec and I are working on, but we've got most of it taken care of now." Our house had been abandoned for a number of years before we purchased it. Finding a dead body in the upstairs bathroom helped us negotiate a lower sales price. Great luck for us, not so much for the dead woman.

She followed me into the kitchen.

"Oh, hello, Lori. Fancy meeting you here," Lucy said.

Lori smiled. "Hello, Lucy. Oh goodness, is that the cake?" Her eyes widened as she moved next to it and leaned in to inhale. "Oh my gosh, I love the smell of lemon. You did a fantastic job with this cake, Allie. I don't even have to taste it to know it's delicious."

"Thank you, I'm glad you approve," I said, and went to the cupboard where I kept bakery boxes. After losing some of my grandma's ceramic pie keepers over the years, I decided I had better invest in some bakery boxes before I lost them all. "It will just take a minute to get it boxed up and ready to go for you."

"How is the dinner coming along?" Lucy asked as she finished cleaning up the counter and tossed the dishcloth into the sink.

Lori crossed her arms in front of herself. "It's coming along wonderfully. I am so blessed to have so many people donate to this event every year. Honestly, I don't know what I would do without it. It's one of our largest fundraisers. All the dogs and cats thank you all for your hard work."

"You are so welcome. I purchased a lovely green glass cake stand to go along with the cake. I was hoping it would help increase the bids." I pointed at the stand sitting on the counter. "I thought it was lovely—nice, simple, and classic."

She nodded. "I think that will work fantastically. And I think you're right; I'm sure people will bid higher to take that cake stand home with them. You're doing a good thing by donating this cake and cake stand. So many dogs and cats in our town are going to benefit from your hard work."

I smiled. It was nice to hear that I was helping a

charity that did so much good in our community. "Anytime you need help, I am more than happy to donate something."

"I'll certainly keep that in mind," she said. "Oh gosh, I almost forgot. I brought your tickets." She opened her purse, dug through it, and quickly produced six tickets: two for Ed and Lucy, two for my son and his wife, Sarah, and two for Alec and me. "That will be a hundred and fifty dollars."

I nodded. It was a lot for a spaghetti dinner, but it was worth it since we knew where the money would go. "I'll get it for you." I headed to the living room where I had left my purse and rummaged through it for the money.

When I returned to the kitchen, Lucy and Lori were laughing about something. "Oh Allie, I appreciate you paying for Ed and me," Lucy said.

I nodded. "It will be a lot of fun." I handed the money over to Lori, and she took it and counted it into her purse, zipping it up quickly. "I sure appreciate this. Now then, what else did you make?"

I hesitated before grabbing the bakery box for the cake. "What else did I make?"

She nodded. "Yes, you offered to make cupcakes, didn't you?"

"But you said you only wanted the lemon pound cake. Did I miss part of the conversation?" I glanced at Lucy, but she looked as confused as I felt.

Lori glanced at the cake and shrugged. "Well, cupcakes would sell so well. I just assumed you would make them. But that's okay if you didn't make any; we don't have to have them."

She may have been saying it was okay that I hadn't made any cupcakes, but her tone suggested otherwise. "I would have made cupcakes if you had told me you wanted them. But it's not too late. I can still make some." It actually was getting rather late to be making fun and fancy cupcakes, but I could manage it.

She waved away the thought. "That's fine, Allie. Don't worry about it. This lovely cake is going to bring in a nice chunk of change for the rescue. As soon as I tell everyone that you're the baker, people will fight over it. I'll have a card with the dessert name and who it was made by next to each item." She chuckled. "Honestly, we've got lots of baked goods to auction off. We don't actually need any more cupcakes. It would have been nice, but we don't have to have them."

I couldn't help but feel like I had let her down, even though I had done exactly what she asked me to do. "Well, I can certainly try to make some cupcakes." I glanced at Lucy, who was looking at me, confused.

"How is the rescue doing?" Lucy suddenly asked.

Lori sighed. "I tell you, starting this rescue and running it is the absolute joy of my life. I couldn't be happier anyplace else. But it's so hard to find good help. People volunteer all the time, but they rarely follow through, and that makes everything so hard. I try to stress to them how important it is to show up when they say they're going to, but it doesn't seem to matter to many of them. I spend so many hours down there, feeding and doing all the things that are necessary to keep the place going, and there are days that it just wears me out. Not that I'm complaining, because like I said, I absolutely love it. I just wish people would follow through on what they say they're going to do."

"That would make things very difficult," I pointed out. "It's a shame that you don't have more help running the place."

She nodded as I placed the cake in the bakery box. "I don't have the funds to hire people. All of my staff are volunteers. Thankfully, we do our best to locate other shelters and rescues that can pick up the dogs and cats and adopt them out—the ones that we can't adopt out ourselves, I mean. So they're not stuck in their cages for a great length of time. That kind of helps, you know?"

"It must still be very difficult," Lucy said. "When you're expecting people to show up once they've promised they will, and they don't follow through, it's just awful."

She sighed again. "Yes, exactly. It breaks my heart when people don't take their volunteer work seriously enough. Little lives are depending on them."

I closed up the bakery box. "I'm so sorry things are hard down there. Maybe Lucy and I could volunteer some time and help you out."

"Oh, that would be fun," Lucy said. "I love puppies and kittens. There's nothing like having happy little furry puppies and kittens around."

Dixie sauntered into the kitchen and, spotting the new arrival, headed over to Lori and rubbed against her leg. Dixie was one of those cats who was laid back and enjoyed company, even if they were strangers.

Lori looked down at him, and for a moment, I thought she would pet him, but she simply slung her purse over her shoulder. "Well, I certainly would appreciate any help you ladies can give. Just call us, and we'll set up a date and time that you can come in and help us out."

I picked up the bakery box. "I'll take this to your car for you if you'd like."

"That's fantastic," she said as she picked up the cake stand, and we headed out of the house. Once I had the cake safely stowed in her trunk, she slammed the lid and turned to me. "Again, thank you for your help, Allie. I appreciate it so much. And don't worry about those cupcakes. Thanks again."

"You're so welcome," I said, and she got into her car. I stood on my front steps and watched her drive away.

If she wanted cupcakes, why didn't she tell me?

CHAPTER 4

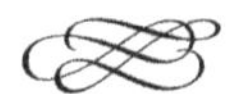

I was sitting in the kitchen enjoying a cup of hot, delicious coffee hoping the caffeine would be strong enough to force my eyelids open for the rest of the day when Dixie suddenly stopped mid-lick of his back leg, tongue sticking out, and stared toward the kitchen doorway. I paused what I was doing and strained my ears to listen. It was Saturday morning, just after seven a.m., and I was getting ready to put cupcakes into bakery boxes. I had stayed up late baking the previous night. Darn that Lori Lynch for not knowing exactly what she wanted. A light knock on the front door came, and I set the box on the kitchen island.

"It's just Lucy," I murmured to Dixie. With this information, he went back to grooming himself.

I headed down the hallway and opened the door. Lucy stood on the front steps, two cups of coffee from the Cup and Bean coffee shop in her hands.

"Good morning, Allie! I thought you might be interested in a vanilla latte." She was entirely too chipper.

I smiled gratefully. "Oh my gosh, you're a lifesaver. The coffee I made wasn't working." I took the cup of coffee from her, and we headed back to the kitchen. "I stayed up until after two a.m. decorating cupcakes. I don't know why Lori insisted she didn't want anything besides the lemon pound cake when I offered to make the cupcakes that day I saw her at Stan's Crab Shack."

"I don't know either," she said. "If I were you, I wouldn't have bothered baking the cupcakes. It's too much work to do at the last minute like that."

I nodded. "I know, but it's for a good cause, and I'm a soft touch."

"Oh, Allie!" Lucy exclaimed when she saw the cupcakes. "They're adorable!"

I smiled. "Thanks. I thought they turned out really well." I had made three dozen chocolate and vanilla cupcakes, each frosted with a large swirly topping of buttercream frosting. Then I piped either a puppy or a kitten face onto each one. I was exhausted after all the work I did, but I was pleased with how they had turned out.

"They are the cutest. They shouldn't have any trouble selling those for five or six dollars at the minimum."

I nodded. "I think they'll do well. There are three dozen of them, so if she sells them individually, I think she'll make more money from them."

I took a big swig of my coffee and began putting cupcakes into a bakery box. We were going to drop these off at the community center where the spaghetti dinner would be held later this evening. I expected Lori would be there, making sure everything was running smoothly. After we dropped them off, we would go for a morning run. I picked up two of the bakery boxes, and Lucy took the other one, and we headed out to her car.

"I'm glad you picked up a vanilla latte for me. I needed the caffeine," I said. I had practically guzzled the whole cup in the few minutes it took us to box up the cupcakes. Now, if it would work its magic, I could keep my eyes open.

"I had them add two extra shots," she said.

I realized it was moments like this when having good friends was important. Lucy always had my back.

* * *

When we pulled up to the community center, I was surprised to see there was only one car in the parking lot. It belonged to Lori. I looked at Lucy. "I expected more people to be here."

"Me too. It's early though. I bet the cooking crew doesn't come in until the afternoon, and the decorating crew will probably be here sometime this morning."

She was right. It still wasn't eight o'clock in the morning yet, and if I knew Lori Lynch, she would have everyone on a schedule. We got out of the car, grabbed the bakery boxes from her trunk, and headed in.

"Do we knock?" Lucy asked.

I shrugged. "If it's unlocked, we'll just go in, and

hopefully we won't startle her." I tried the door handle, but it didn't budge. "Oh."

"Knock."

I knocked on the heavy double door and we waited, but Lori didn't open it. I knocked again, harder this time, but still got no answer. I turned to Lucy. "Maybe we should try going around the other side. Oh wait, I've got her phone number. Hold on." I shuffled the two bakery boxes onto the one she was holding and rummaged through my purse for my phone. When I found it, I hit dial on her name. The phone rang several times, and I looked at Lucy.

"Not answering? Maybe she's in the middle of something and can't get to her phone."

I let the call go to voicemail, then hit end and called her again. But there still was no answer. I hit end, and shrugged. "You're probably right. Let's see if we can find another door. If it's closer to wherever she's working, she may hear us knock."

We headed around to the side of the building, and I knocked loudly on the first door we came to. After waiting for several minutes and knocking two more times, we moved on, hoping to find another one.

"I wonder what she's working on?" Lucy said. "If

nobody else is here to help her decorate or cook, what would she be doing here this early?"

"I don't know. She strikes me as being a bit of a control freak, so it doesn't surprise me that she's here to look things over. If the room doesn't pass muster with her, heads will roll." We both giggled as we came to another door. I knocked on this one, but again, there was no answer.

I groaned. "She has to be here. That was her car out front, wasn't it?" I tried to look over my shoulder, but I couldn't see the car from where we stood.

"I'm pretty sure that's her car. It's very nice and looks expensive."

She wasn't wrong. Lori drove a modern luxury sedan. One of those streamlined cars that, at first glance, doesn't scream opulence, but when you take a closer look, it's clear that a pretty penny was paid for it.

"Maybe we should go by the Cup and Bean and get another coffee. That first one isn't doing much, and I need more of a boost," I said. "When we get back, she may be in a place where she can hear us knock." I was getting a little uneasy about the situation.

"We could do that," she said. "But I hate driving

around with cupcakes in my trunk. What if I slam on the brakes? What if they fly across the trunk and get smashed up? All that hard work for nothing."

"Yeah, as much work as I put into them, I don't want to see them get ruined." And then a thought occurred to me. "What if she was here last night and was working on decorating the place and for some reason she got a ride home? Maybe her car broke down? Or maybe her husband came in his car and they both went home together?"

She nodded. "They may have gone out to dinner and just left her car here. He's probably going to drop her off here this morning, and she'll have her car to drive home when she's ready."

It sounded plausible, but I wasn't sure about it. "Let's see if we can find one more door to knock on first."

"Sounds good."

We rounded the corner of the building and there was a set of double doors in the back. When I got to them, I knocked as hard as I could, but the place remained eerily silent.

I knocked again and when no one answered, I tried the handle and was surprised when it gave. "It's open," I hissed.

"Oh, thank goodness, these cupcakes are getting heavy."

"I'm so sorry. I should have taken those two boxes back."

"It's okay, you can't knock on doors and carry cupcakes, too."

I took the two top boxes from her. There were lights on inside and the door opened up to the kitchen. There were bags of groceries sitting out on the counter. "See, she was here last night. Look at all this food."

"It's a lot of food," Lucy said. "I bet they're going to have a huge crowd tonight."

I nodded, and we set the bakery boxes on the kitchen counter. I glanced over the bags of groceries and then at the large industrial-sized refrigerators along one wall.

"I wonder where the desserts are? She wanted to gather them up so she could bring them down here herself. I don't know why she didn't just have everyone bring everything first thing this morning."

Lucy nodded. "I think that would have been a better idea. Her going to pick them up and then bringing them down here was an extra set of hands touching everything and there is always the possibility that something might get dropped."

"Let's try this room over here and see if we can find her. Lori?" I called. I didn't want to sneak up behind her and startle her.

The open door led to a room that was set up with round tables covered in white tablecloths.

"Oh, this will be nice," Lucy said, trailing off.

We both spotted Lori at the same time. Lucy and I turned to look at each other, our eyes wide. We ran across the room.

Lori was sitting at a long table where several desserts had been set out, including my lemon pound cake. And Lori was sitting in a chair with her face smashed into my cake. The sight was so shocking it was hard to think about what I needed to do.

"Lori?" Lucy whispered.

I hurried around to the other side of the table and pulled her back to a sitting position onto her chair, lifting her head from the cake. I tried to feel for a pulse, knowing it was too late. That was when I noticed the blood on the back of her head. "Oh, Lori," I said. I grabbed my phone from my purse and dialed Alec, as Lori slumped forward, face on my cake again.

When he answered, I said, "Alec, Lori Lynch is dead."

There was a pause. "What do you mean, dead? Where are you?"

I took a deep breath. "We're down at the community center. Lucy and I came down here to bring the cupcakes for the dinner, and we just found Lori face down in my lemon pound cake."

"She's dead?" he asked.

"She's dead all right." I looked up at Lucy. Her eyes were wide, and she stared at Lori's cake-covered face.

"I'll be right there. Don't touch a thing," Alec said.

He didn't have to tell me twice.

CHAPTER 5

Lucy and I stood off to the side and watched as Alec began photographing the scene. I felt bad for Lori as she lay there in my cake, unmoving. Alec glanced up at me. "No one else was here when you got here?"

I shook my head. "No, there was no one else here. Lori's car was parked outside, and we didn't see anybody else."

"Oh gosh," Lucy said, turning to me. "You don't suppose that the killer was running out the front door while we were coming in the back, do you?"

I hadn't considered this. "I hope not." I looked at Alec. "Has she been dead long?"

He shook his head. "No, rigor mortis hasn't set in yet."

I took a deep breath. Of course, it hadn't. I had easily moved her back to a sitting position when we first found her. The thought of the killer possibly being inside the building at the same time we were made my blood run cold. "That makes me feel a little ill."

Lucy swallowed. "Me too."

"Yancy and Bill are clearing the rest of the building," he said as he knelt to examine something on the floor. "If the killer left in a hurry, they may have left something behind."

"We knocked on several of the other doors, trying to get Lori to open for us," I said. "So, if the killer was still here in the building, they knew we were here."

He nodded without looking at me. "If they were still in here, I'm sure the knocking scared them off."

I crossed my arms. "I hate to even think it. And poor Lori. Who on earth would hit her in the back of the head like that? And why would they do it over my cake?"

Alec glanced up at me, one eyebrow raised. "That seems a little odd, doesn't it? Maybe they were trying to send you a message."

I knew he was teasing, but it still made me protest. "Alec, I don't know any killers. At least, I hope not."

He chuckled as he continued his work. "There are no signs of a struggle, so she may have known her killer and let them in."

The thought made me sad. Was her killer a loved one? Or rather, someone who she thought was a loved one?

Yancy entered from one of the other hallways with Bill on his heels. "The building is cleared and secured," he said to Alec. "We've got backup on the way."

Alec gave a curt nod of his head. "The coroner should be here soon."

I doubted it. Brant Olney was the slowest person on the face of the earth. And then I thought of something. "What are we going to do about the dinner tonight? Volunteers are going to be arriving to decorate and cook."

"There won't be any dinner here tonight," Alec said without looking at me.

"Oh, that's awful," Lucy said. "The animal rescue needs the funds to keep operating. This fundraiser is crucial."

Alec stood up. "I know they do, but we have a situation on our hands and the fundraiser will not happen tonight."

Lucy sighed. I leaned toward her and nudged her. When she looked at me, I nodded my head toward the kitchen, and we headed that way.

Inside the kitchen, Lucy turned to me. "What do you have in mind?"

I shrugged. "Let's just take a look around and see if we notice anything." Lucy and I had investigated a crime scene or two before. And while Alec didn't necessarily approve of that, he was usually tolerant of it. I tore two paper towels from the roll by the sink and handed one to her, then I went to the industrial-sized refrigerators and used my paper towel to open the door. Inside sat an assortment of desserts that were supposed to be auctioned off tonight. "Will you look at that?"

"Look at what?" Lucy said, hurrying over to my side.

"Lori sure asked a lot of people to bring desserts. I could have easily made several more, and she wouldn't have had to run around trying to find people to bake something."

She shook her head. "Didn't she know she had the world-famous Allie Blanchard at her fingertips?"

I turned and eyed her. "Apparently not."

We carefully looked over the kitchen, but it was spic and span, just as we had expected it to be. The groceries were still sitting in their bags on the counter, except for the refrigerated items that had been stowed away. There didn't appear to be anything out of place, but what had the murderer used to kill Lori with? I turned to Lucy. "What in this kitchen would be heavy enough to kill someone with?"

"A stockpot?"

I shook my head. "A stockpot would be too large and awkward. Think smaller and heavier. It didn't appear as if they had struck her multiple times, so it has to be heavy." I was no medical examiner, but if the killer had hit her more than a handful of times, the back of her head would have shown it.

She nodded and went to one of the cupboards and opened it. "Maybe there's some cast iron cookware here. Those things are really heavy."

I nodded, but the cupboards revealed stainless steel cookware. I picked up a frying pan, but it wasn't nearly heavy enough. Unless the killer was extremely strong. I set it back down, and stood up. "They may have taken the murder weapon with them."

She nodded, and we turned to go back to where

Alec was still examining the crime scene, but Lucy stopped at the doorway. "What about a meat tenderizer? You know, one of those mallet things?"

I turned to her. "Do you think it would be heavy enough?"

She nodded. "I do. And if the killer was strong enough, it wouldn't take many blows. At least I don't think it would."

We went back to the cupboards and searched for a meat tenderizer but couldn't find one. After several minutes, I said, "I think they took it with them. I mean, if there was even one here to begin with."

"I bet it's the murder weapon," Lucy said.

We turned and headed back to the dining room. Lori was still sitting face-first in my cake. The green glass cake stand had fallen on its side, and the cake was in an awkward position, partially resting on the stand, with the rest beneath Lori's face. "Did you find her purse?" I asked Alec.

He looked up at me, squinted, and shook his head. "Not yet. Did you?"

I shook my head. "No. And a woman always carries her purse."

"It could be in her car," Lucy said.

"Maybe. But she was planning on being inside the

building for a long time, and that meant her purse was vulnerable in the car, even if she hid it out of sight and locked the car up. Somebody might have broken in and stolen it. But it's worth taking a look."

"Got it, chief," Alec said. "We will take a look."

I frowned. "Don't make fun of me."

He shook his head without looking at me. "I'm not making fun of you. As soon as I finish up here, we'll go over everything, and then the two of you will be free to leave."

But I didn't want to leave. There had to be more clues here. My eyes traveled over the dessert table. It appeared that Lori had just started setting the desserts out. There were only nine cakes, including mine. Each one had a neatly typed card in front of it with the name of the dessert and the name of the baker, just as Lori had said there would be. In the table's corner was a neatly stacked deck of index cards for the rest of the desserts in the refrigerator. I looked it over and that was when I spotted a card sitting on the table with no dessert behind it. I moved over to get a closer look at it. It said, 'coconut cake, baked by Anna Dawson.' Lucy came to look at the card with me, and after she read it, we both turned to look at each other.

"Where's the coconut cake?" she whispered.

I shook my head, and we hurried back to the kitchen. "Maybe she set the card out first and didn't get a chance to bring the cake to the table."

"She may have been getting ready to do that after setting your cake out. I bet that's why she ended up face-first in your cake."

I nodded. That made sense. I flung the refrigerator door open that contained the desserts, and we quickly took inventory of what was there. When we had carefully looked at all the desserts, we turned to each other again. "There's no coconut cake here."

She nodded. "The killer stole the coconut cake."

We stared at each other.

"Come on," I said, closing the refrigerator door. We hurried back out to Alec. "Alec, someone stole the coconut cake."

He looked up at me, a puzzled look on his face. "And?"

I nodded. "Look. She was setting the cards and the desserts out one by one. There's a card for coconut cake, but no coconut cake. It's not in the refrigerator, either."

He considered this for a moment and then nodded.

"Unless Anna Dawson didn't bring the cake yet," Lucy said.

I shook my head. "No, I don't think that's what happened. Lori was very meticulous. She wouldn't have set all the cards on the table and then gone to get the desserts. No, she was taking each cake and each card individually and setting them out. That card wouldn't be on the table unless she had set the cake on the table as well. Plus, she was picking the desserts up herself." I felt triumphant in what I had put together.

"You're right," she said.

I nodded. "Okay then, we'll talk to Anna Dawson and see what she has to say."

Lucy added, "Let's go see if we can find anything around Lori's car."

"I would appreciate it if you two wouldn't mess with stuff," Alec said sternly. "And I'm about finished here, so we need to go over everything."

"We'll be right back," I said. "We won't be but a moment."

Lucy and I headed out front as more police officers arrived. "How's it going, Yancey?" I asked. Yancey Tucker had been a fixture of the Sandy Harbor Police

Department for as long as I could remember. He was tall and thin, and he looked harried now.

"Oh, I guess it's going all right. What are you two up to? Alec said you found the body."

I was about to answer when movement caught my eye. I turned as a line of six cars pulled into the parking lot. The troops had arrived to prepare for the event.

CHAPTER 6

Anna Dawson was the first to exit her car. Her eyes darted from the police cars to the community center, then back to the police cars. Anna was Lori Lynch's assistant at the animal rescue. She wore jeans and a black T-shirt, her long brown hair pulled back in a simple ponytail. There wasn't a speck of makeup on her face. Anna was in her mid-30s, and what my grandmother would call pleasingly plump. The athletic shoes on her feet were grungy and I could see a small toe poking out of the hole in the side of the left one. Her eyes were wide, and she smiled in a way that said she was unsure of what to make of the police presence.

Yancey sidled up beside me, hitching a thumb into

his belt. "We can't have you folks in there today," he said with a curt nod of his head.

Anna's eyes widened. "But we have a dinner to put on. What's going on, Yancey?"

He shook his head. "There won't be any dinner, I'm afraid. No one is to cross that line." He jerked a thumb back at the building without turning around. There was no police tape put up yet, but I saw an officer grab a roll from his car.

She looked past him. "What line?"

He glanced over his shoulder, then turned back. "There's about to be a line of police tape around this entire building. I know you all were counting on setting up this fundraiser, but it isn't going to happen today."

She stood in front of her car, unsure of what to do, and glanced at me. "Hey, Allie, Lucy. What's going on?"

I smiled. "I'm afraid there's been a hitch in the plans for the fundraiser."

She put her hands on her hips. "Okay, but *what* is going on? What happened that we can no longer have the fundraiser dinner tonight? Lori will be furious when she hears this. You can't just shut us down at the last minute." She glanced over her shoulder. "Wait a minute, that's Lori's car, isn't it? Is she here? I bet she threw a fit when you told her she couldn't hold her fundraiser." Her eyebrows knit together.

"I'm afraid Lori doesn't have much choice about it," Lucy said.

"What's that supposed to mean?" Anna asked as two other women walked up behind her.

"What's going on?" asked the tall blonde woman. She looked vaguely familiar, but I couldn't place her.

"Why is he putting up crime scene tape?" Miriam Davis, the other woman with her asked. "What happened?"

"That's what I want to know," Anna said. "Yancey, what's going on?"

Yancey sighed. "Ladies, I hate to break it to you, but there's been a crime committed, and we're not at liberty to say what happened."

"I heard they only put that kind of tape up when there's been a murder," the tall woman said. "Is that what happened? Was somebody murdered?"

Anna's eyes widened in understanding. "That's what happened, isn't it?"

Yancey shook his head and held both hands up in front of himself, palms out. "Now look, I can't discuss police business. You ladies are going to have to clear out." By this time, four others had walked up to us.

"There's been a murder?" Cynthia Donaldson asked. "Is that what I heard?"

"It's Lori, isn't it?" Anna asked suspiciously. "That's her car in the parking lot. It has to be her."

Yancey made a face. "Like I said, you all are going to have to clear out. You'll have to figure out what to do about the fundraiser on your own. I need you to leave."

Anna turned to me. "Allie, what's going on? Lori was murdered, wasn't she? How awful. I can't believe somebody would murder her." She shook her head.

"Oh, no, that's horrible," Cynthia said as the others muttered in disbelief.

I shifted my weight from one foot to the other. Until Lori's next of kin were notified, the police weren't going to say a word, and I knew Alec would expect me to keep my mouth shut. "I really don't know much of anything. But as Yancey said, there won't be a fundraiser tonight."

Anna glanced at the front door of the community center as the officer strung up the crime scene tape. "It's a murder, all right. They wouldn't use that tape otherwise. What happened to her?" She was looking at me now, and I just shrugged and shook my head.

I glanced at Lucy. "I'm not at liberty to say anything."

Yancey sighed. "What am I going to have to do to get you ladies to leave?"

It took several more warnings from Yancey to get most of the ladies to clear out. Anna stayed behind.

I turned to Yancey. "I suppose we'll get going now, Yancey."

He nodded. "See you later, Allie."

Lucy and I walked slowly toward my car, and Anna tagged along.

"What happened, Allie?" Anna asked. "Your husband is in there, isn't he?"

"Anna, you know Allie isn't able to tell you anything," Lucy said.

She groaned. "Oh, come on, you know I won't say anything to anyone."

I turned to Anna as we walked. "Lucy and I were just bringing some cupcakes down for the fundraiser tonight. I had already given Lori my lemon pound cake last night, but I decided I should make some cupcakes to help raise more money for the cats and dogs. The job that you all do down at the animal rescue is so important, and I was hoping the cupcakes would help raise even more money to help you continue doing what you do."

"I agree," Lucy said, nodding. "It's an important job, and we in the community really appreciate it."

Anna sighed. "We try to do our best to save as many cats and dogs as we can. We've even saved a few hamsters and guinea pigs over the last several years. This fundraiser is so important to us to keep things running smoothly. Without it, we couldn't do nearly as much as we do. What did you see inside? You got inside, didn't you?"

"Anna, did you make something for the silent auction after the dinner?" I asked, ignoring her question.

She nodded. "Oh, of course. I always make something for the silent auction. This year I made a triple-layer coconut cake. My mother used the same recipe to win at the county fair years ago. It's moist and delicious and so coconutty."

That was odd. There was a card on the table with her name on it and the coconut cake listed, but no coconut cake. When Lucy and I had searched through the refrigerator, I was certain there was no three-layer coconut cake in there. It would have stood out because it would have been taller than the others. "Did Lori drop by your house and pick it up to bring it down here?"

She nodded as we stopped at my car, and Lucy leaned against it. "Oh yes, she made the rounds and picked up most of the desserts." She rolled her eyes. "I don't know why she insisted on doing things that way; it would have been so much easier if she had allowed everyone to bring their desserts down here. But that was Lori. She insisted that things be done a certain way, and you better believe it was going to be done that way." She was quiet for a moment, then her eyes widened. "Oh gosh, listen to me. I'm talking about her in the past tense. She's not really dead, is she?"

I hesitated. I wasn't going to give out more information than Alec would have wanted me to. "I wonder why she wanted to pick up everything herself? You're right, it would have been easier to have everyone bring their donations down here."

"She would have had to make a lot of trips back and forth," Lucy pointed out.

She sighed. "Lori was a control freak, like I said. She wanted to personally look over each of the desserts being auctioned off. Just between the three of us, she also wanted to check out the homes of the people doing the baking."

My eyes widened. "What do you mean?"

She shook her head. "She wanted to make sure that the house the food had been made in was clean."

I gasped. "She thought the people's houses wouldn't be clean?"

She nodded. "Lori looked down on people. Sometimes people would volunteer to bake something for the sale, and she was sure that their homes wouldn't be clean enough, so she would make sure to drop by and pick up the baked goods. If the house didn't pass muster, she would dump the baked goods."

"But wouldn't the person who had made the donation wonder where their item was if it wasn't at the auction?" Lucy asked.

She nodded. "Yes, then she would just tell that person that somebody came in and was so excited to buy what they had made that they offered her a large donation for it. She would even write up one of those cards she usually makes for each baked good and leave it on the table to make them believe what she was saying was true. And of course, she couldn't divulge who the person was who bought it, because they wouldn't want their personal information disclosed."

Well, that was one way of doing things. "I suppose she was just trying to be kind."

She shook her head. "No, she didn't want anybody to get sick from something they bought from our fundraiser. And while she would have liked to just tell people their house was too filthy to accept baked goods from, she realized it might hurt her image if she came off as an unkind person. And believe me, Lori was an unkind person. There were many instances where she would say something wretched to people."

I had a feeling that Anna may have been one of those people. "Did you get along with Lori?"

She sighed. "Lori is the most insufferable person I've ever worked for. She left all the dirty work to me while she floated around attending dinners and holding fundraisers and doing all the things that wouldn't cause her to get her hands dirty."

I believed every word she was saying. Lori was always dressed nicely, with her hair and makeup done. But Anna was dressed as if she knew what hard work was all about. "She was unkind to you?"

She nodded, avoiding eye contact. "I kept telling

myself that I shouldn't take things personally. Because Lori is just one of those people who thinks more highly of themselves than anyone else. She was self-centered."

"But at least she wanted to help the cats and dogs," Lucy pointed out.

Anna smirked. "She wanted people to see her as a kind, giving person. Most people have a soft place in their hearts for cats and dogs, and seeing Lori provide a service of rescuing animals in peril made them think she was a good person."

I gazed at Anna as I took this in. If what she was saying was true, then somebody may have become angry about her not wanting to sell their baked goods at her auction. And Anna's cake was missing.

CHAPTER 7

Alec wouldn't be home until late, so I took advantage of the time alone to make him a wonderful dinner of barbecued spareribs, corn on the cob, and grilled veggies. Usually, Alec did the barbecuing, but since he was going to be working late, I decided to surprise him. It was the timing I was worried about. I would have liked to get the timing down so that the food would still be hot from the grill by the time he walked through the door, but I knew that was going to be tricky.

For dessert, I made him lemon pound cake since the one I had made for the fundraiser had gone to waste. Never mind the cupcakes—we had left them on the counter in the kitchen at the community center, but at least those wouldn't go to waste. After I got home, I remembered them and texted Alec to let him know that he and the other officers were more than welcome to help themselves. They would be at the murder scene for hours, and the cupcakes would at least help their flagging energy later.

Dixie rubbed up against my legs as I hovered near the barbecue to make sure nothing burned. I glanced down at him. "I know you smell these ribs, but I'm not making them for you."

He looked up at me and meowed.

"Well, maybe there will be some leftovers. I know you like to chew on a good bone, so there will be that."

He rubbed his face against my leg, and I reached down and scratched his ear. My life had been enriched by owning a cat, although sometimes I wondered if he owned me. Lori Lynch had been doing a good thing with her animal rescue. She had told me once that she drove all over the state of Maine to pick up cats and dogs that were in danger of being euthanized at county shelters and took them to other rescues where they could be adopted. And then, of course, she had adoptions right here in Sandy Harbor. I hated to think about what might have happened to Dixie otherwise. She had rescued him first, and then I rescued him and gave him his forever home. "Would someone want to kill a woman who was doing important work like rescuing animals?"

Dixie meowed at me.

"You clearly don't know the answer to that question either, do you?" I stood up, closed the lid to the barbecue, and sat down on a lounge chair. The weather this summer had been mild, but that didn't stop me from consuming copious amounts of iced sweet tea.

* * *

"Dinner smells delicious," Alec said when I opened the oven door where I had been keeping the food warm at a low temperature. It was just after eight o'clock, and I was happy he could come home earlier than I had imagined he would.

"I hope it hasn't gotten dry." I stood up on tiptoe and kissed him. "I miss you when you're gone all day."

He pulled me to him and kissed me. "I miss you too. And I'm starving."

He released me, and I got some plates and set them on the table while he got glasses of iced sweet tea for us. "So, how goes the investigation?"

He shook his head. "There was no trace of Lori's purse." He turned and looked at me. "We went through her car when we found her keys in the kitchen, but no purse."

I nodded and got the pan with the ribs, taking them to the table. "I told you she wouldn't leave her purse in her car like that. She had to have brought it in, and the killer must have stolen it. Do you think that means this was a simple robbery? Maybe they noticed the back door was open. She may have been bringing some desserts into the building from her car and propped it open."

"That's a possibility," he said, setting the glasses of sweet tea on the table. "But until we do some more investigating, it's going to be hard to say."

I got the grilled vegetables and brought them to the table next. "What about that coconut cake? Did you ever find it?"

He shook his head and sat down at the table. "No, there was no coconut cake. Not in the trash and not in the refrigerators. Maybe she made the card up and then realized the cake hadn't been brought yet."

I nodded and sat down, placing two ribs on my plate. Dixie was under the table, waiting for me to sit so he could rub against my legs in the hopes of a tasty morsel being tossed his way. "I guess that's possible. But it makes me wonder about what Anna Dawson said about Lori tossing the desserts if she felt the donor's house wasn't clean enough. There's a part of me that thinks that's petty, and there's a part of me that thinks that's smart." I shrugged and unfolded my napkin.

He looked at me with one eyebrow raised. "I suppose people are safer not eating food from certain people's homes." Then he chuckled. "I never really thought about it if you want to know the truth."

"Me either. And I wonder if Anna Dawson is someone who Lori thought no one would want to eat her food. Lucy and I should probably stop by her house and take a look for ourselves." Throwing away food that had been donated to a fundraiser was crass, but since it was Lori Lynch we were talking about, it wasn't surprising.

He shook his head. "I don't want the two of you getting into any trouble."

I smirked. "Trouble? Why would Lucy and I get into trouble? You know us better than that. We'll stay out of trouble." At least I hoped we would. "Anna and Lori are very different people. Lori loved attention, and she always dressed to get it. But Anna doesn't seem to want any attention, and she dresses for work."

"Do you think Anna did most of the work at the rescue?" He put three spareribs on his plate, followed by a large serving of grilled vegetables and an ear of corn.

I nudged the butter across the table to him. "I would almost bet on it. I think that's what Anna was trying to get across without sounding like she was bragging about herself when she was complaining about Lori. And I can't really blame her. Lori got all the attention for the rescue, but I can't imagine her scooping litter boxes or cleaning up after the dogs."

He slathered butter on his corn. "That might have been frustrating for Anna. She had to do the dirty work while Lori got all the attention." He looked at me. "Do you think that makes her a suspect?"

"Did you get a chance to talk to her?"

He shook his head. "Not yet. I'm going to drop by the rescue tomorrow and take a look around and talk to people there. If Anna was jealous of the attention Lori got, perhaps she got tired of it."

"Honestly, it wouldn't be a surprise. Not that I think Anna really had something to do with the murder, but people like Lori can be hard to take. She loved talking about herself and really enjoyed the attention. If it wasn't Anna, then it wouldn't be surprising if it was somebody else she worked with. Someone who was tired of doing the dirty work while Lori kept her hands clean and got all the praise." I didn't know if I was jumping to conclusions or not. But knowing Lori, I could see where somebody would get aggravated with her and decide to put an end to it.

He picked up his barbecue spareribs and took a bite, then nodded appreciatively and gave me a thumbs up. When he had swallowed, he said, "These are delicious. Nice and tender and juicy. I should let you barbecue more often."

I grinned. "I don't think they're as good as if you had made them, but I think they turned out well. Did you get a chance to talk to Lori's husband?"

He nodded. "Yes, I went by to talk to him and tell him about his wife. He was broken up over it, of course."

"Did he give you anything to go on? Was he shocked at the news?"

He nodded. "Yes, Alan Lynch seemed stunned by the news. He said he couldn't think of anyone who would want to kill his wife. He kept saying he just couldn't believe it."

"With an event as large as this fundraiser was, why wasn't he there helping her?" if it were me, Alec would have been there every step of the way.

"He said he was going to be there with her at the fundraiser. He always attended them and helped her with whatever needed to be done during the event. But he said he works a lot of hours at his office and doesn't have a much time to help her with things that need to be done in the lead-up to an event like this."

"I forget. What does he do for a living?" I put some butter on my grilled vegetables and my corn. Dixie rubbed harder against my legs, insisting that I not forget him.

"He's a lawyer. He specializes in family law."

"I guess I can see that he would be busy then, like most lawyers."

He nodded and speared some grilled zucchini onto his fork. "He says he frequently works on the weekends and late into the evening. But he had no idea who might have wanted to kill his wife."

I sighed. "It's a shame he didn't have any ideas. But

since family members are always the first people that you look at, how do you feel about him?"

He shook his head. "Like I said, he seemed genuinely shocked that someone had killed his wife. Until I get some evidence that says he may have had something to do with it, I'm going to consider him genuinely grieving his wife's death."

I took a sip of my sweet tea. "Then we had better either find some evidence that says he did it or find some that says somebody else did it."

I slipped Dixie a small piece of meat as I thought this over. Lucy and I needed to pay Lori's husband a visit, too.

CHAPTER 8

Lucy and I dropped by the Cup and Bean coffee shop the following morning after our run. "That was a good run," I said.

Lucy turned to look at me. Her short blond hair stuck to her forehead with sweat. "Yeah, I guess."

I eyed her. "What do you mean, you guess? We made good time, and I'm not as worn out as I usually am." Some of our runs were shorter and easier, while others were longer. We were working on building up our stamina, and today had been a long run.

"My legs feel like jelly. It wasn't an easy run for me."

"Really? I'm so sorry because I feel pretty good."

We got out of my car and headed up to the Cup and Bean.

She shook her head. "I've been staying up too late at night and not getting enough rest. I think that's what it is."

I held the door open for her. "That's probably it. You've got to get to bed early enough so your muscles can rest."

There was no one standing in line, so we hurried up to the counter before somebody decided they needed to place an order and jumped in front of us. I looked up at the menu board, then turned to the barista. "I'd like a vanilla latte and a strawberry muffin, please."

"I'd like the same," Lucy said.

I nodded and paid for our lattes and muffins.

Our old friend, Mr. Winters, sat at a corner table, looking over his newspaper. We headed over to him. "Good morning, Mr. Winters," I said.

He looked up from the newspaper. "Good morning, ladies. How goes it?" We sat in the chairs across from him, and I bent beneath the table and patted his little gray poodle, Sadie. "It's going great. How about you?"

He shook his head. "Plumbing is leaking again. I've got a plumber coming to see about it later."

"Oh no," Lucy said. "I hate plumbing trouble."

"Me too." He turned to me. "Red, I heard there was a murder. Is that right?"

I nodded and leaned forward. "Yes, Lori Lynch. Do you know her?"

He nodded again. "Sure, who doesn't know Lori Lynch? She runs the animal rescue and sticks her nose in everyone's business. Everyone in town knows her."

I felt my eyes widen. "She sticks her nose in everyone's business?"

He nodded. "Sure, she's a busybody. But it's a small town, and I suppose there are many busybodies running around." He winked.

"Oh sure, that's probably true," Lucy said and took a sip of her latte. "What do you know about the murder?"

He folded his newspaper and leaned over the table again. "Not much. For her being such a busybody, people are feigning ignorance. But I have my own ideas." He took a sip of his black coffee.

"Well, don't keep us in suspense. What are your ideas?" I asked.

He eyed me before answering. "It's important work, running that animal rescue. Everybody in the community gets behind it whenever she needs anything. Like that fundraiser that was supposed to be held on Saturday. People volunteer to help, donate something, or even give her a little cash for it. And she raises enough money to keep the rescue going. People like her on that basis alone. But the ones who know her, I mean, really know her—some of them might not like her as well because she's a gossip. She's also controlling, and if she finds out something about you, she'll use it to her advantage. And she'll tell you how to run your life." He chuckled.

Maybe I shouldn't have been surprised at this, because I knew she was controlling and liked to tell people what to do. I chalked most of that up to the fact that she owned and ran the animal rescue. She was a woman in charge of making sure that little furry lives were saved, and she was no-nonsense where that was concerned. I couldn't fault her for that. "Go on."

He took another sip of his black coffee. "Coffee is cold. Need another cup."

"I've got it." Lucy jumped to her feet and grabbed

his cup. "Don't start until I get back." She hurried to the front counter to get a refill for Mr. Winters.

He looked at me and chuckled. "I like that one. Service with a smile."

I shook my head. "Mr. Winters, you are incorrigible."

Lucy was back before Mr. Winters could even straighten out his thoughts to continue telling us what he wanted to share. "Thanks, Lucy. Now, as I was saying, if you keep your ears open, you'll hear lots of complaints about Lori Lynch. But I usually dismiss things like that, this being a small town and all. But one thing I know for sure is that she was having an affair with Jeremy Winthrop."

I gasped. "Jeremy Winthrop? How do you know that?"

He shrugged. "Doesn't everyone know that?"

I shook my head. "No. I didn't know that."

"I didn't know that either, so everyone doesn't know," Lucy said. "Do you know that for a fact?"

"They've been seeing one another for years. I even saw them check into that little motel on the outskirts of town a couple of years ago. In the middle of the afternoon." He whispered the last part.

I stared at him, stunned. "I had no idea. Mr.

Winthrop still owns the real estate company, doesn't he?"

He nodded. "He does. Also, he's Lori Lynch's biggest donor. At least, according to him, he is."

"Well, I'll be," Lucy said. "He's making donations, *and* he's having an affair with her?"

"Yes, apparently he's her biggest supporter in more ways than one. I asked him once whether he was an animal lover, and he said no. As you can imagine, I was shocked. I asked him why he would give her so much money to rescue animals if he didn't care about them. He said she twisted his arm, and it was easier to donate than to listen to her complain about needing money. And besides that, he could write it off on his taxes."

"That doesn't sound right," Lucy said. "Nobody donates to a charity because the person running the charity nags them." She turned to me. "Does that sound right to you?"

I shook my head. "No, that doesn't make sense. Unless he really is having that affair with her, and it would affect their relationship if he didn't."

"Of course they're having an affair," Mr. Winters said. "Do you think I would make up something like that?"

I took a sip of my latte. "No, I don't think you would make up something like that. But something about it seems odd. I wonder if her husband knew she was having an affair?"

He shrugged. "I have no idea, but since it was going on for a lot of years, you would have thought he would have gotten wind of it and put an end to it." He looked at me. "Maybe that's what he did. Maybe her husband put an end to their affair by killing her."

It was possible. "Or maybe there was something behind Lori's complaints about not having enough money for the rescue. Maybe she was threatening Jeremy Winthrop and making him pay up. "

Lucy nodded. "Blackmail."

This was interesting. "Did he ever mention how much money he gave her?"

"No, he never mentioned how much." He took a sip of his coffee. "But you've got to figure that running an animal rescue like that costs a lot of money. There's food, cat litter, rent or a mortgage to pay, utilities, and transportation fees. Not to mention if any of the animals are sick, they need veterinary care and medicine. I took Sadie to the vet two months ago when she had a sinus infection, and it cost me almost three hundred dollars. Now multiply that by, I don't know, however many animals she was helping, and it gets expensive."

"It would be very expensive," Lucy agreed.

"But there's something else," he said, taking another sip of his coffee before continuing. "Jeremy Winthrop doesn't even try to hide the fact that he thinks Lori was spending his donation inappropriately, and that he felt like he had no other choice but to donate."

"You mean, he thought Lori was using the funds for something other than helping the animals?" Lucy asked.

He nodded.

"Blackmail," I whispered.

Lucy turned to me. "I bet that's what it was. He felt like he had to give her that money, and it doesn't sound like it was because he loved her."

I shook my head. "No, he sounds resentful about it, and there has to be a reason for that."

"Resentful is right," Mr. Winters said.

This was important information, and I had a hunch it was going to lead to something big.

Mr. Winters reached beneath the table and petted Sadie. "I wish I could say I knew what was behind it all, but I can't. I have a feeling if we put our heads together and search for answers, we'll come up with something big, though."

"You can say that again," I said. In the past, Mr. Winters had given us information that helped solve murder cases. I was sure he could come up with something that would be helpful in this case, too.

I took another sip of my latte, taking this in. Did Lori's husband know about this affair? If he did, why would he allow it to go on? Had he just recently found out about it and put an end to it by ending his wife's life? I felt like that couldn't be it. How could they have kept a long-running affair quiet? In this town, people liked to talk, and somebody would have discovered the affair and probably let him know about it.

CHAPTER 9

We waited three more days before dropping by Alan Lynch's home. I had whipped up some lemon blueberry muffins to bring to him.

"These muffins smell delicious," Lucy said as she held the bakery box.

"I made a lemon glaze to put on the top of them, and I think they turned out really well."

"I'm sure they did."

I parked in front of the Lynch's home and gazed up at the house. It was a modern two-story with a white picket fence. The yard had planter boxes along the front and yellow and pink flowers danced gracefully in the light afternoon breeze.

"I love their house," Lucy said as we got out. "It looks big."

"Doesn't it, though? I'm sure it's beautiful inside. I would expect nothing less from Lori Lynch."

I knocked on the door, and we waited. When no one answered, I rang the doorbell. A moment later, the door slowly opened, and a young woman poked her head out. She looked puzzled to see us standing there.

I smiled. "Hello, you must be Katie. My name is Allie, and this is Lucy. We just wanted to stop by and tell you and your dad how sorry we are for your loss." As I was saying this, it occurred to me that I didn't know if this was Katie or not.

Her eyes widened, and for a moment, I thought I had made a mistake. "Thank you. Let me get my dad." She closed the door and was gone.

"I'm glad you knew who that was," Lucy whispered.

I nodded. "Lori spoke of Katie often." She told me Katie was in her first year of college studying to be a doctor when I ran into her at the grocery store last fall.

The door opened again, and Alan Lynch stood there, dressed in a pink T-shirt and faded jeans. His feet were in white socks, and he smiled sadly. "Oh, hello, Allie. Hello, Lucy."

I smiled again. "Hello, Alan. Lucy and I just wanted to stop by and tell you how sorry we are about Lori."

"Yes, we are so very sorry for your loss," Lucy echoed.

"I appreciate hearing that. I can't imagine what we are going to do without Lori." Katie crowded in behind him, peeking over his arm that held the door open.

"I can't begin to imagine what you must be going through." I glanced at Lucy. "Oh gosh, I almost forgot. I was baking last night, so I made you some lemon blueberry muffins." Lucy held the box out to him.

He took the box from Lucy. "That's so thoughtful of you, Allie. Thank you. Would you ladies like to come in?"

"We would love to," I said. We followed him inside, and just as I thought, the house was beautifully decorated with a light blue sofa and loveseat, and large paintings of flowers and pastoral scenes hanging on the walls. The coffee table and side tables were intricately carved dark wood.

"Why don't you ladies have a seat?" He gestured to the loveseat, and Lucy and I sat down. He sat across from us on the couch while Katie hovered awkwardly nearby.

"You have a lovely home," Lucy said.

Alan was tall and balding with deep laugh lines etched across his face. He sat back on the couch and crossed his legs. "Thank you. I'd like to take credit for it, but it was all Lori. She planned every detail of this house and bought only the best of the best. Personally, I would have been fine with lawn chairs and a folding table." He laughed. "That's why she handled it all. She knew what I would pick out."

I smiled. "Some people have a knack for decorating, and some people just don't."

He laughed again. "I'm one of those who don't." He took a deep breath and sobered. "I talked to your husband the other day. I hope he finds my wife's killer soon because if he doesn't, I will, and they will be sorry."

"I know he will do everything he can to find them quickly. But you mustn't do anything rash. It won't be good for you or your daughter." I glanced at Katie, who was still standing off to the side. She had long, straight blonde hair and wore black-framed glasses.

She was cute in that awkward way that teenagers have.

He shook his head. "I'm not going to do anything stupid. But I haven't gotten a wink of sleep since I found out about Lori. Something has to be done."

"Alan, what time did Lori get to the community center? Did she say she was meeting anyone there?" I asked. I knew he had already told Alec these things, but I hoped that if I could get him talking, he might remember something he forgot to tell Alec.

"No one was supposed to show up until later, and she left the house at about 5:45 a.m. Can you believe it? I told her there was no reason for her to be there that early, but she was a perfectionist. Just like with this house, she wanted that fundraiser to be executed perfectly. She's the same way with the animal rescue. All the kennels, crates, and cages have to be perfectly clean at all times, and the animals have to be fed at precisely 6 a.m. and 6 p.m. I don't blame her for demanding that everything be perfectly cleaned, but she was down there all the time fussing about everything. I told her that was what she had Anna Dawson for." He shook his head.

"I'm sure it's a lot of work taking care of all those

animals," Lucy said. "I can imagine why she would be so worried about them. I would be that way too."

He nodded. "Yes, but she had Anna supervising all of that. She should have just let her do her job."

"Did Lori and Anna get along?" I asked, hoping my question didn't sound too pointed.

He shrugged. "I guess so. I mean, she was always complaining that Anna wasn't doing things right, but I figured it was because she was demanding too much of her. We know all about that, don't we, Katie?"

At the sound of her name, Katie jumped a bit. Her eyes widened, and she quickly nodded. "Yes, mother could be very demanding."

I looked at her. *Mother?* It was a rather formal title for someone who had nurtured her and presumably been close to her all her life.

I smiled at Katie. She had the look of a deer caught in headlights. "I'm so sorry for your loss, Katie. I imagine this is so hard to deal with."

She nodded. "Yes, I think I'm still in shock."

"Whenever I ran into your mother around town, she almost always brought up your name and told me how proud she was of you. The fact that you were going to become a doctor delighted her," I said gently.

Katie stared at me in silence for a moment. "She did? She talked about me?"

I nodded. "Oh yes, she was so proud of you. She said that you graduated near the top of your class in high school, and she was so pleased." Why did this seem to surprise her?

Katie's eyes darted to her father, and then back to me. "Yeah, my mother was very supportive of me and my school career."

It sounded hollow when she said it.

"It's wonderful having a supportive mother, isn't it?" Lucy asked. "My mother was always so encouraging of me."

She nodded again and blinked.

"Katie, why don't you get the ladies some coffee?" Alan said.

She nodded again. "I'll be right back with coffee."

"You must be so proud of her, Alan," I said when she had left the room.

He nodded. "Yes, Katie is the apple of my eye. I'm afraid she's still in shock over the death of her mother, though. Lori loved our daughter so much. I remember when she found out she was pregnant with her. She didn't sleep for a week; she was so excited."

Hearing him say that made me feel better about

Katie's response to what I had said. "It's wonderful when a child is wanted so much."

"It sounds like you all were so close," Lucy said. "I love to hear about families like yours."

He nodded, looking away. "But now it's all over. Someone killed my wife, and our family has been destroyed."

My heart went out to him. Losing a spouse in such a terrible, violent way would not only destroy the family unit, but it would be something that would take a long time to work through. "I'm so sorry."

He looked up at me with tears in his eyes. "All I want is justice for my wife. I need that. I need your husband to find her killer. Now."

"He will," I said, hoping I wasn't promising something Alec couldn't deliver. Some cases went cold, and I hoped this would not be one of them.

He gave a curt nod of his head. "I have faith in him."

Katie returned to the room with a tray full of cups of coffee, cream, and sugar. She set it on the coffee table with a jerk, causing the cups to rattle against one another. "Here we are."

"Thank you for the coffee, Katie," Lucy said.

She straightened up and smiled. "You're welcome. I hope you like it. It's Colombian coffee."

I picked up a cup. "I'm sure it's delicious. Katie, how are you doing?"

She frowned and fidgeted with her hands as she stood there. "I'm doing okay. I miss my mother, of course, but I'm trying to remember the good times."

"That will help you get through this," Lucy said, stirring sugar into her cup. "I sometimes feel that when you remember the good things about a person who has passed, it sort of brings them back to life, if you know what I mean."

Katie nodded. "I think you might be right. I feel like my mother knows when I'm thinking about her."

We sat and visited with them for a while longer, and when we finished our coffee, we left.

I started the car and turned to Lucy. "Katie seems like an odd girl."

"Tell me about it. She calls Lori Mother. Not Mom, or Mama, or any number of casual names."

I nodded as I pulled away. "Very odd."

CHAPTER 10

"Do you suppose he's in?" Lucy asked as we sat in her car, looking at the Winthrop Real Estate Agency.

I shrugged. "There's only one way to find out."

"Let's go, then," she said. We got out of the car.

The Winthrop Real Estate Agency was one of the largest and probably most successful real estate agencies in the area. I wasn't sure how many people worked there, but I thought there had to be at least five or six real estate agents. I didn't think Jeremy sold houses anymore; rather, he was the businessman behind the business.

I pushed the door open and was greeted with a blast of cool air. The day had turned warm, and it felt good on my face. I smiled at the blonde at the front desk.

She looked up at me and flashed movie-star white teeth. "Good afternoon, ladies. Do you have an appointment?"

I shook my head. "No, we don't have an appointment, but we were wondering if Mr. Winthrop was around."

Her brow furrowed slightly. "Mr. Winthrop? Yes, he's here, but he doesn't see visitors without an appointment. Can I make one for you for another day?"

"We'd rather just see if he's available," I said, glancing around the office. Everything was neat and tidy, and there were certificates of achievement on the back wall.

"Oh, I'm sorry, but as I said, he doesn't take visitors without appointments. But I would be happy to set one up for you." She started tapping on her keyboard. "He's available next Friday."

"Is he with a client now?" Lucy asked.

The young woman smiled, but I could see annoyance building around the edges. "I'm sorry, maybe I could just take your names and phone numbers? I'll make sure he gets them with the message that you stopped by. Or we can make an appointment."

I sighed. I had hoped we would get to talk to him for a bit. Making an appointment made our questioning seem more official, and we were anything but official. Just as I was going to tell her not to worry about it, I heard a door down the hallway close, and in a moment, Jeremy stepped out of the hallway. I smiled. "Hello, Jeremy. How are you doing?"

At the sound of my voice, he looked up, and a puzzled look crossed his face for a moment. He smiled. "Good afternoon." He glanced at Lucy. "Allie. Lucy. Don't tell me the two of you are looking for new houses?"

"Not exactly," I said, glancing at the blonde. She seemed perturbed that we were going to get to speak to him anyway, despite her efforts. "I really hate to bother you, Jeremy, but do you have a few minutes?"

He hesitated, then nodded. "Sure, I guess I've got a few minutes. I've got a customer coming in, but it won't be for another ten minutes or so. It won't take any longer than that, will it?"

I shook my head. "No, ten minutes is perfect." I was feeling a little excited now. We were going to get to speak to him, and I wondered what he could tell us about Lori's last days. He was tall, with a medium build, and he was completely bald. He had to be at least eight or nine inches taller than Lori, and that would put him at the perfect height to hit her in the back of the head and kill her. Was he her killer?

He nodded and handed a file to his receptionist. "I got everything I needed on this. You can file it away."

She smiled up at him in an admiring way. "I certainly will, Mr. Winthrop. Please let me know if there's anything else I can do for you."

He gave her a lopsided smile, then turned back to Lucy and me. "Why don't you come on back?"

We nodded and followed him down the hallway to his office. It was more spacious than I expected, with a few green plants here and there and a carved mahogany desk in the center of the room. We sat down on the padded chairs he indicated, and he went to sit behind his desk. "What can I do for you ladies?"

I put my hands in my lap, trying to come up with a way to ask him the questions I needed to ask. "How are you doing, Jeremy? It's been forever since I've seen you around town. You must be so busy."

He smiled. "Business has been good. Houses are selling like hotcakes and at prices I didn't think I would ever see."

"Houses are so expensive these days," Lucy agreed. "Business must be very good for you."

He nodded. "It's always nice to see business pick up."

"How many real estate agents do you have employed here now?" she asked. "I always wanted to be a real estate agent, but it seems like something always got in the way, and I never got the training to become one."

"Oh, that's a shame." He glanced at the clock on the wall. "I think it's one of the most exciting jobs around. You get to meet so many interesting people, and the pay isn't bad." He winked. "But to answer your question, I've got five real estate agents working for me now. Are the two of you in the market for a house?"

I shook my head. "Not exactly. Jeremy, I heard you were a donor for the Fluffs and Stuffs Rescue. I'm sure you've probably already heard about what happened to Lori Lynch?"

His brow furrowed, and he nodded. "Yes, what a shame. I can't imagine who would have wanted to murder her. What did you want to see me about?"

I shrugged. "We were just in the neighborhood, and I remembered hearing you donated money to her cause, and I thought I would stop in and say hello."

He looked uncertain now. "Who told you I was a donor?"

I hesitated. I couldn't tell him that Mr. Winters had found this information out. "You did. I think it was a year ago when we stopped to talk at the grocery store. You mentioned how much you enjoyed giving to the animal rescue."

He nodded at this information. "Oh, yes. I enjoy donating money for that kind of thing. Although, between the three of us, I'm not sure Lori Lynch was the right person to be running the rescue. It's nothing against her, but she just didn't seem the type. She hated getting her hands dirty, and I heard she rarely did. To be honest, I don't know why she would have gotten involved in an animal rescue."

"She didn't seem the type, did she?" Lucy agreed.

"No, she didn't. She told me she couldn't stand the smell of the animals when it rained. She said she tried to stay away from there when that happened. I told her it rains a lot around here, so I guess she didn't show up much." He chuckled.

"I wonder why she would run a rescue like that if

she wasn't that fond of the animals?" I asked. "It sounds like she wasn't fond of them."

He shrugged. "I think that's an excellent question. She never really had a straight answer when I asked her. Honestly, I didn't care much for her, and I'm surprised she had any interest in rescuing animals."

This surprised me. Wasn't he having an affair with her? Gossip traveled quickly in this town, so maybe that's all it was. But Mr. Winters had also said that he didn't like animals, and yet he said he did. "Did you go by the rescue often?"

He shook his head. "No, not often. I got my Shih Tzu from Lori a couple of years ago. I didn't know what I was looking for at the time, so I paid a couple of visits to the rescue, and when I laid eyes on Mitzi, I knew she was the dog for me." He chuckled. "I suppose that sounds silly—a man like me with a little dog like that. But she was a sweet dog, and I couldn't leave her there."

"Oh, she does sound sweet," Lucy said. "I was thinking about going to the shelter to pick out a dog, but I've never gotten around to it. Plus, I don't know how my husband would react to me bringing one home."

"You should take him down there, and you can

both look them over. Your life is never the same once you adopt a dog." He smiled and glanced at the clock again. We didn't have much time.

"Was Lori there when you went to pick out your dog?" I asked. Was this how they began their affair? If there was an affair, that is.

He nodded. "Oh sure, she was there. Honestly, she was there each of the few times I've been there. But I could tell by the look on her face that she really didn't like the animals. She constantly complained about them and about how much it was costing her. She twisted my arm to get me to donate money to the rescue, and then when I did, she insisted I give her more. It was a never-ending thing with her. Always wanting more money."

"And did you give it to her?" I asked. "More money?"

He sighed. "Yes, I gave it to her. What else was I going to do? She would make me feel guilty for not doing it. Like it would be all my fault that the dogs and cats would starve to death without me making donations." He rolled his eyes. "But I can take it off my taxes, so it's not like I had a reason not to do it."

"It's good to make donations to a charity like a

rescue," Lucy said. "I'm sure it costs a lot of money to take care of the animals."

He sat back in his chair, gazing at us. "I don't know who would have killed Lori, but I was very close to reporting her to the police for neglect of those animals. Some of them were skinny, and others needed medical attention. She claimed they came to her like that, but it seemed like a large number of them weren't being taken care of."

"That's surprising," I said. "I wouldn't have thought that of her." If she was the perfectionist I believed her to be, it would have carried over to how she took care of the animals. Her husband had even said she was that way with the animals, as well as everything else in her life.

He snorted. "Lori made sure that people saw what she wanted them to see. I will not miss having to deal with her. She called me frequently, demanding that I increase my donations, and it was annoying."

"So you spoke with her frequently? Why would she feel she could demand that of you?" I wondered out loud.

He rolled his eyes. "Almost every day. I think she thought the world revolved around her, and that's why she thought she could be so demanding."

Lucy frowned. "She called every day? She was bothering you about donations every day?"

He hesitated and shook his head. "That's an exaggeration. Not every day. But frequently."

But I thought it probably was every day, especially if they were having an affair. "Were you close to Lori?"

He gazed at me again. "I've got an appointment. They'll be here any moment. If you ladies will excuse me."

His eyes met mine, and I tried to read the truth in them, but I couldn't see anything there. I stood up. "Thank you for your time, Jeremy."

We showed ourselves out of the office, with the blonde ignoring us as we walked past. When we got back in my car, Lucy turned to me. "Was he talking to her on an almost daily basis because she wanted more money for the rescue?"

"No, she was talking to him every day because they had a relationship."

CHAPTER 11

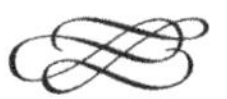

"Oh, my goodness, Lilly, look at how tall you're getting!" I swept my granddaughter into my arms and gave her kisses while she giggled hysterically. She had gone from an infant to a toddler lickety-split, and I wasn't sure how I felt about it.

"Look at Lilly getting kisses from her Mimi," my daughter-in-law Sarah said. "She loves her Mimi."

"Of course she's getting kisses from her Mimi; she's the sweetest thing in the entire world," I said, balancing her on my hip.

"What about kisses for her granddad?" Alec asked.

I scooted over and leaned toward him, and Lilly leaned back and giggled at him. He leaned over and gave her a quick kiss on the cheek. "You'll be signed up for ballet class before we know it."

"I can hardly wait," I said. "Pink tutus and tiaras."

Lucy held her arms out to Lilly. "Her Auntie Lucy needs her now."

Reluctantly, I handed her over to Lucy. Lucy kissed her cheek, and Lilly just ate it up.

I had invited Lucy and Ed, and my son Thad and his family for dinner. We were barbecuing steaks and burgers, and the house smelled delicious from the barbecue out on the patio.

"Steaks are almost done," Thad said, entering the house from the sliding glass doors. "Oh hey, Ed, Lucy. Nice to see you."

Ed gave Lilly a quick kiss on the cheek. "Good to see you too, Thad. What's new?"

Thad shook his head, a barbecue tong in one hand. "Just enjoying the summer off."

Ed nodded. "I hear you. Teachers gotta enjoy their time off while they can." Thad and Sarah were teachers at the local high school. Having two months off during the summer was exciting for them.

Lilly squealed when Lucy tickled her.

"Lilly's going to be so wired by the time y'all get home; she'll never go to sleep tonight," I said.

"That's okay, she loves being around family." Sarah was chopping the vegetables for the salad.

"You'll think otherwise when she screams in the middle of the night because she can't sleep," Lucy said. "Not that I'm going to stop tickling her, though."

"I think everything is just about ready for dinner." I looked up as Jennifer entered the kitchen. "Hey, Jennifer, how come you didn't invite your boyfriend?"

Jennifer smiled. "Soon. Someday soon, you'll get to meet him."

"Oh, I can't wait," Sarah said. "What's he like?"

"He's cute," Jennifer chuckled. "I only date cute guys."

I watched my daughter as she grinned and giggled. I love to see my family happy.

"Jennifer, if you could get some glasses and fill them with ice, that would be wonderful." I went to the refrigerator, and got the potato salad I made earlier in the day, and brought it to the table.

"I'd help you, Allie, but my hands are full," Lucy said as she tickled Lilly.

I smiled. "That's okay. Some things are more important than others."

We got to work putting the food, iced tea, and lemonade on the table. Thad went out to get the steaks and burgers off the grill, and the doorbell rang. "I'll get it." I turned and headed down the hallway to the front door. When I opened it, I was surprised to see Mr. Winters standing there. "Hey there, Mr. Winters. How are you doing this evening?"

His eyes were wide, and he had his little dog on a leash. "Allie, I found out the most horrible news today. Can I come in?"

"Of course you can. Come on in, we were just getting ready to eat. Would you like to join us? We barbecued steaks and burgers." I led the way back to the kitchen, wondering what horrible news he had heard.

"I heard from Diana Lane that the animal rescue sold cats and dogs to the lab over in Vermont."

I gasped and spun around. "What? What do you mean they sold cats and dogs to the lab? What kind of lab?" I became aware that the kitchen had gone silent behind me.

He nodded, and Sadie sat at his feet. "Yes. Apparently, Lori Lynch was selling cats and dogs to a medical testing lab over in Vermont. I couldn't believe it when she told me."

Alec turned to him. "Who is Diana Lane?"

"She runs the nail salon by the grocery store," Mr. Winters said.

Lucy shook her head. "That's horrible."

"It's worse than horrible," Sarah said. "It's—I don't know, it's just the worst thing I've ever heard."

I caught Dixie sneaking into the kitchen to check out Sadie from the corner of my eye, but I ignored him. "How does she know this?"

He shook his head. "She said that everybody knew this, but when I told her I didn't know, she just shrugged. She said if we would check around, we would find out that a lot of people know about it."

"None of the people I've interviewed about the murder have mentioned this," Alec pointed out. "It seems like with Lori's murder, someone would have brought that up."

I nodded. "I agree. I've never heard anything about her selling animals to a lab. Has anyone else?" I glanced around at everybody standing in the kitchen, and they all shook their heads.

"Steaks and burgers coming right up," Thad said, carrying a platter of meat into the kitchen. He glanced around at us and then noticed Mr. Winters. "Mr. Winters. You made it just in time for dinner."

"Yes, your mother has invited me, and those steaks

smell absolutely divine." Sadie wagged her tail at his feet, hoping that the invite was extended to her as well.

"What's going on? Everybody looks like they've seen a ghost," Thad said as he set the platter on the table.

"Mr. Winters just told us that Lori Lynch's animal rescue sold cats and dogs to a lab in Vermont for medical testing," I said.

His eyes widened. "She wouldn't do that, would she?"

Mr. Winters shrugged. "All I know is what Diana Lane told me. But she insisted other people around town knew about it."

I went to the table and sat down, motioning for everybody else to do the same. "Well, none of us have heard anything about it. Maybe she's wrong." I couldn't imagine that kind of news not being spread far and wide if it was true.

"I certainly hope she's wrong," Lucy said, sitting across from me after handing Lilly off to her mother to put into the highchair. "It's a horrible, horrible thing."

"And then doing fundraisers to collect money too?" Ed said. "She was the lowest of the low if that's what she was doing. No wonder someone murdered her."

He had a point. If Lori truly had been selling these animals to the lab and then collecting money on the side, she really was the lowest of the low. I turned to Alec. "What do you think?"

He shook his head as he sat beside me. "I'll have to dig into this. But if it's true, maybe it shouldn't be so surprising that she ended up murdered."

"Especially since they murdered her on the day of a big fundraiser. Maybe they were trying to send a message," Jennifer said.

Sadie yelped suddenly, as Dixie took a swipe at her tail.

"Dixie! You leave Sadie alone," I said and got up.

"I'll put him in another room," Thad said. He scooped the cat up, taking him down the hallway.

"Sorry about that, Mr. Winters. Dixie doesn't get much non-human company." I sat back down.

Mr. Winters chuckled. "That's okay. All he did was tap her tail."

I placed some salad on my plate, shaking my head. "I hope Lori wasn't doing that. The thought of it makes me sick."

"I'm with you," Lucy said. "What a horrible thing

to do. I think we should go down to the rescue and look around. Don't you think so?"

I nodded. "That's a great idea. Maybe we'll see some evidence that says she did that. You know, Lucy, you and Ed should get a little dog or a cat. Give some wonderful little fur baby a home."

"That's a great idea," Lucy said, her eyes widening as she put potato salad on her plate. "What do you think, Ed?"

He shook his head. "No, I don't want a dog or a cat. How about we get a snake?"

Lucy made a face. "We are not getting a snake. Absolutely not. I want something warm and fuzzy that I can snuggle up with."

"You can snuggle up with a snake. It would probably appreciate the warmth," Ed said, placing a steak on his plate.

Lucy rolled her eyes. "Oh, you. But we should think about this. We haven't had a pet in years, not since Smokey died."

Ed nodded. "Smokey was a good little dog, but if you've got a dog, you really can't go anywhere with them. What if we wanted to travel?"

"We never go anywhere," Lucy pointed out. "We could get a cat. If we went someplace for the weekend, we could put extra food and water out for it, and it would be fine left alone for a couple of days."

"It's settled then. You're getting a cat," I said. "You'll love it. They're so much fun." Except when they were sneaking up on your guest's dog.

"We should get a cat," Sarah said to Thad.

Thad nodded his head at Lilly. "We've already got a warm little creature running around the house. I think that's enough for now."

"Oh," Sarah said. "I think Lilly would love a cat. We should think about it."

I cut into my steak. "Those poor little kitties down at the rescue are just waiting for somebody to come and rescue them. Everybody should get a cat."

Mr. Winters helped himself to a steak. "I already rescued Sadie. I don't need a cat."

I chuckled. Mr. Winters had indeed rescued Sadie when her previous owner was murdered. He had done a wonderful thing for the little poodle.

I hoped it wasn't true about Lori Lynch selling animals to the lab. It was unthinkable.

CHAPTER 12

When I woke up the next morning, I was still stunned by what Mr. Winters had told us about Lori Lynch and her animal rescue. In my heart of hearts, I didn't believe Lori was selling sweet cats and dogs to a lab for medical experiments. But there was another part of me that wondered if it might be true.

We drove by the Cup and Bean drive-through and grabbed an iced coffee on our way out to the animal rescue. It was just outside of town and had kennels inside and outside, along with large play yards for the dogs. Shade trees grew along the fence lines to give the dogs plenty of shade during the summer.

"I just can't believe it's true," Lucy said, taking a sip of her iced coffee.

I nodded. "Frankly, I'm stunned. If it's true, I'll be heartbroken."

"Me too."

There were several other vehicles in the parking lot when we got there and a family with a little girl carrying a brown, mixed-breed puppy was exiting the building as we were headed inside.

"Oh," Lucy said, drawing the word out. "Isn't that sweet?"

I nodded. "That's exactly what this rescue is for—to find families for sweet little puppies and kittens. Have you decided whether you're going to get a dog or a cat?"

She shook her head and held the door open for me. "Ed said he doesn't want a dog."

"We'll have to get a cat for you, then," I said.

She chuckled. "Well, he didn't say I couldn't have a cat. And they pretty much take care of themselves, so why not? But we'll just look around and see what they've got today. I don't want to jump into it too quickly."

I nodded as an older man shuffled up to the counter when he saw us. "Can I help you?" He wore a khaki-colored button-down shirt with the name 'Gerald' embroidered on a patch on the upper left side.

I nodded. "We'd like to look at your cats, please. Do you have any kittens?"

"Follow me." He came around the counter, and we followed him through large swinging doors. "We've always got kittens. Plenty of kittens."

We followed Gerald down the center aisle amid the cacophony of barking dogs. Big dogs, little dogs, and some medium-sized dogs were thrown in just for good measure.

"Oh, they're all so sweet," Lucy said as we looked over the dogs we passed. "You really need to get a dog," I said, and pointed out a cocker spaniel. "Look at that. Isn't he sweet?"

She nodded as the dog wagged his stubby little tail. "He's just gorgeous. I wonder how he ended up in a place like this. How could his owners have gotten rid of him?"

I shook my head. "I don't know. He needs a little grooming, and he would be the perfect picture of what a cocker spaniel should look like."

Gerald glanced back over his shoulder. "That cocker came to us from a family who dropped him off. He belonged to their grandmother, but she passed away, and none of them could take him home."

My heart melted. "Oh no. I hope he finds a home."

"Me too," Lucy said, looking longingly at the cocker. "Maybe I don't care so much about what Ed thinks about getting a dog after all."

We moved on to a wall that had cages with cats and kittens in them. "Oh wow, there are so many of them. I didn't think you kept this many here," I said to Gerald.

He shook his head without turning around and then stopped in front of the cages. "We just got a bunch of new ones in. They were going to be euthanized at the county shelter, but Lori arranged for transport before she passed."

"We were so sorry to hear what happened to Lori," I said sympathetically. "I still can't get over it. How are you doing, Gerald? It must be so hard, having your boss die like that."

He shrugged but didn't look terribly upset. "We're doing fine here. We've got too many cats and dogs to look after to worry about what happened to Lori."

I was surprised at his answer. "You do have a lot of animals. But aren't you the least bit concerned about how she died? It was murder, after all." By this time, the news had gotten all over town about someone murdering Lori.

He nodded. "Yeah, it's a shame. But not much changes around here for us. You know?"

I shook my head. "No, I don't think I do know. What are you talking about?" He said it like I wasn't the smartest person around.

"Lori never did much of anything around here. She arranged for transport sometimes, but mostly it was left to Anna or me. But she liked to dress up and raise funds for the rescue, so I guess I can't complain too much."

"Raising funds is important," Lucy pointed out as she stuck her finger into the cage that held a Siamese kitten. "Aren't you cute?"

He sighed. "Yeah, without funds, we aren't gonna get far. We'll have to figure out how to take care of that now that she's gone."

"Did you like working for Lori?" I asked.

He grimaced. "Did I like working for her? What kind of question is that? No. I hated working for her. She wasn't the nicest person, and she was lazy."

"Then why did you stay? If you're a volunteer, there must be other things you could volunteer to do around town." I stuck my finger into a cage and petted a little black kitten, who was begging for attention.

"I'm not a volunteer. Anna and I are the only paid employees. Everybody else is a volunteer." He glanced over at a woman wearing an orange T-shirt, who walked a dog on a leash out the back door. "We've got fifteen to twenty volunteers, depending on the time of year. People don't like to volunteer much when it's snowing, so we have more of them during the summer."

"That's a lot of volunteers," Lucy said. "Thank goodness you have a lot of help."

He shook his head. "It's not a lot when you consider that most people only want to put in an hour or two once a week. I guess it makes them feel good to volunteer, but we need them here more often than that and for a longer time frame. That's why we have to have so many volunteers."

"But I was under the impression that sometimes there aren't any animals here. Like after you've transferred them to another rescue." The black kitten was so darn cute, and I wondered how Dixie would feel about having a little brother or sister.

"Sure, but that doesn't last long. Maybe a day or two. So many dogs and cats need homes." He reached over to the cage and opened it for me so I could pick up the kitten.

"You are too sweet," I said, holding the kitten close.

There were three other kittens in the cage with the black one, and they scurried over to the open door, but Gerald closed it before they could fall out. "Especially kittens. There are so many kittens."

I looked at Gerald's face. It was lined with age, but there was something else too. He truly cared for these animals. "It's a good thing they have you and Anna to look after them."

His eyes darted to meet mine, and then he looked away. "But that Lori, she didn't care much about the animals. She wouldn't get her hands dirty for anything."

"How can you say she didn't care about the animals?" Lucy asked, running a finger over the kitten's head. "She had to care about them to have started up this rescue. It had to cost a lot of money to get this place going."

Lucy had a good point. These buildings didn't just pop up overnight; it would have cost a lot of money to have the place built.

He shook his head. "No, there was another organization here that was running something similar to what Lori was doing. They only took care of dogs. Lori added the cats to the mix. That organization ran out of funding and Lori was able to talk her way into taking the place over. They still own the property and the buildings, and Lori was making rent payments to them. She said she got a good deal though, and it wasn't expensive because that organization was happy that somebody was going to move in and continue their work."

"That sounds like a good deal," I said. Lucy took the black kitten from me. "Lucy, you need that kitten."

"I think *you* need this kitten. I've got my eye on that little calico over there." She pointed at the cage beneath the one the black kitten had come from.

Gerald stepped up and opened the cage door, and Lucy reached in and picked up the calico, holding two kittens now. "Aren't you the cutest? I swear, I couldn't work in a place like this because it would be too heartbreaking not knowing if the animals that left here were really going to have a good home."

Our eyes met, and I knew what she was talking about. I turned to him. "Gerald, you sound like you really care about these animals. I really respect that."

He gave a quick nod of his head. "Sure, I care about them. I don't like hearing about any animals being harmed."

"Will you answer something for me? I heard a rumor going around town that Lori was selling these dogs and cats to a lab over in Vermont for medical testing. Is that true?"

He looked at me, his eyes widening, but he just stared, saying nothing. My stomach dropped. *Was it true?*

Suddenly, he shook his head violently. "No. That isn't true. Do you want a kitten or not? We've got paperwork to fill out if you do."

Lucy and I looked at each other, both of us taken aback by the abrupt change in his manner. "I think we just want to look at them today. We need a little time to think things over. They'll be here for a while, won't they?" I asked.

"We've got a rescue coming in tomorrow to pick up some dogs, but as far as I know, the cats will be here for a few more days. But don't wait too long or you'll miss out on them." He swung open the doors to the cages, and Lucy put the kittens back. He closed them and motioned toward the front door. We headed back out front with Gerald walking behind us.

"We'll probably be back," I said over my shoulder as we left.

"I don't like the sound of that," Lucy said. "I think they are selling them to labs."

I shook my head. "I don't. I think Gerald cares too much about these animals." I hoped I was right.

CHAPTER 13

After we left the shelter, we picked up an iced coffee for Alec and drove over to the police station. I was going to get more than my share of caffeine today.

Joe Denning was sitting at the front desk when we walked in. He smiled, then frowned. "Good afternoon, Allie. Afternoon, Lucy," he nodded. "I bet you're wondering why I'm frowning."

"Why are you frowning, Joe?" I asked. I had an idea what the answer would be.

"Because I don't see a bakery box in your hands." He sighed dramatically.

"I'm so sorry, Joe. I've got to make something for you wonderful officers here at the station. You keep us safe, and you deserve a treat for that." I tried to keep the officers supplied with treats, but it had been a while since I brought them anything.

"I told her she needed to make something and bring it down to you all," Lucy said innocently.

I elbowed her. She was lying. "I promise it will be soon."

He chuckled. "I look forward to it. Do you wanna go back and see Alec?"

I nodded and headed toward the door that separated the offices from the reception area. "You know I do."

"Go on back."

He buzzed us through, and we headed down the hallway that led to Alec's office.

"Hey, Allie!" Ben Tiller, the chief of police, hollered from his office as we passed.

I slowed down and smiled at him. "Ben, how have you been? And how is Anita? We've got to get together soon and do something fun."

He nodded. "Anita and I were just talking about that the other day. Let's not wait too long."

"We won't," I said and hurried to Alec's door. I knocked quickly and opened the door before he hollered for us to come in.

He looked up from his laptop, surprised to see us. "Well, hello there. How are you girls doing today?"

We stepped into his office, and I closed the door behind us. "Alec, I think Lori really might have been selling cats and dogs through the rescue." I set his iced coffee in front of him on his desk, and we sat down in the chairs in front of it.

"It's awful," Lucy said, taking a sip of her coffee. "I just can't imagine how she could be so horrible as to do something like that."

"What makes you think that's really happening?" he asked, taking a sip of his coffee. He nodded approvingly. "This is good."

"We went down there and had a look around. We spoke to someone named Gerald who worked there. When I asked him about the rumor, you should have seen the look on his face. It really made me wonder if it was true," I said. I was waffling back and forth on whether I believed it was happening or not.

"Gerald who?" he asked.

I shook my head. "We don't know. But the name on his uniform was Gerald."

"And he didn't seem to like Lori all that much," Lucy added. "He really couldn't stand her."

"You didn't get his last name?" Alec asked.

"No, we were just acting like we were interested in the animals. Oh, and Alec, there was an adorable black kitten down there. I'm seriously thinking that Dixie needs a new brother or sister. I didn't even check to see if it was a boy or a girl, but it was the cutest thing. We need another cat." My leg jiggled, and I took a sip of my coffee. This was my second one of the day and the caffeine was kicking in.

"I don't know that we need another cat," he said. "What did the place look like? I was planning to go tomorrow morning and have a look around."

"The place looked fine," Lucy said. "It wasn't bad at all. No overcrowding, and the animals all looked healthy. I was looking at a calico kitten, although there was the cutest little cocker spaniel in the kennels."

Alec chuckled. "Do you think Ed is going to agree to a pet? He doesn't strike me as an animal person."

She shrugged. "He might not get a vote. It would be so much fun to have a furry little friend at the house. I always pet Dixie when I come to your house, but I don't have a cat of my own."

He nodded. "I think you should get one. Everybody needs a little four-legged friend."

"Two four-legged friends are even better," I pointed out.

He chuckled. "If you really want another cat, I'm fine with it. But I don't know how Dixie is going to feel about it. He's been top dog, or rather top cat, for years and he may not want to share the attention with anyone."

"I didn't think about that. But I think after an initial adjustment, he'll be fine." At least I hoped he would be fine. Sometimes cats didn't get along. Dixie might not have the patience for a kitten.

"Okay, but if things don't work out, what are you going to do?" He took a sip of his iced coffee and sat back in his chair.

"I haven't thought of that," I said. I couldn't imagine bringing a kitten home only to find out Dixie couldn't adjust and then have to take it back to the rescue. It would break my heart, not to mention breaking the kitten's heart.

"What are you going to do if the rescue really is selling cats and dogs to a medical lab?" Lucy asked him.

He thought about it for a moment, then shook his head. "I don't know. I'd have to look into the legalities of it to see if we could do anything. I don't know if there's anything illegal about it."

My heart sank. I wanted him to say that he was going to shut the place down. "There's still an excellent chance it's not happening, but you didn't see the look on Gerald's face. He didn't want to answer my question about it."

"He looked surprised that we knew about it," Lucy agreed.

Alec jotted a note on a piece of paper. "I'll have to do some research and see what I can find out. Did Mr. Winters say the lab was in Vermont?"

I nodded. "He said Vermont."

He looked up at me. "Maybe there's some law about transporting animals across state lines to sell to labs. I doubt it, but I'll look."

I sighed. "I guess if that's all you can do."

"That's all I can do until I find an answer. There may be something in the law about selling them from a rescue shelter. It seems a bit deceiving to me to get people to donate to a charity like that and then to have the animals sent to a lab for a profit instead of helping them to find a home."

"Yes, it's very deceptive. A lot of people were helping

with that fundraiser, and many people also made cash donations. They didn't do that for the animals to be shipped somewhere to be experimented on. I will be so angry if it's happening. I've always thought those animals were being found loving homes." I couldn't stand the thought of the animals being treated that way. Then I thought of something and gasped.

"What?" Alec asked.

"What if somebody was making regular, large donations to the rescue and then discovered that not only was Lori taking that money from them, but was also selling the animals to the lab for even more money? That would make that person angry, wouldn't it? Angry enough to kill her."

Lucy turned to me. "And Jeremy Winthrop is her biggest supporter."

I nodded. "And he's having an affair with her." My mind started spinning. Jeremy had to be the killer, didn't he?

"Now, let's not jump to conclusions," Alec said. "We don't know for sure that Jeremy was having an affair with her or that he was her biggest donor. Mr. Winters doesn't have proof of that, right?"

I shook my head. "No, I don't think he has proof."

"Until we have evidence of those things, and

confirmation of the animals being sold to a lab, we can't do anything about it. But it's something I will look into," he said.

I knew he was right. Without ironclad proof, there wasn't a lot he could do. We needed to find that proof.

"How is the investigation going?" I asked.

"I was talking to Lori's husband this morning, and he said he's been getting phone calls from a blocked number. No one ever says anything when he answers, and they hang up after listening for a few seconds."

"That sounds scary," I said. "I wonder if it's the killer? And if it is, why would they be calling him?"

Lucy nodded knowingly. "I bet they're just trying to harass him. People can be so cruel. First, they killed his wife, and now they're going to torment him by making these phone calls."

"That's terrible," I said. "Has he given you any additional information about who might have killed Lori? Sometimes people remember things when they've had time to think about it."

He shook his head. "No, he swears he doesn't know who would want to kill his wife."

"Poor Lori." Then I thought for a moment. "Okay, not poor Lori if she's selling little animals to a lab to be experimented on. Horrible Lori, if that's what she was doing."

"I can think of all kinds of things to call her if she was guilty of that," Lucy agreed.

We talked to Alec for a few more minutes before leaving him so he could get back to work. I hoped he could find information about whether it was legal for Lori to have sold the animals if that was indeed what she had done.

CHAPTER 14

The knock on my front door startled me. "Who could that be?" I muttered as I went to answer it. I was surprised to find Katie Lynch standing on my step, looking like a scared rabbit.

I smiled. "Well, good morning, Katie. How are you doing?"

She looked up at me. Her glasses made her eyes look three times bigger than they were. "Good morning, Allie."

I waited for her to say something else, but I realized she might need some help. "What brings you to my neck of the woods?"

She took a deep breath. "Oh, I don't know. I've got

to go." She spun around as if to head back to her car, but she stopped.

"Katie, would you like to come in? I've made coffee and lemon blueberry muffins. Did you get a chance to try any of the muffins I brought to your house? I thought they turned out nice and moist."

She took a deep breath and turned back to me. "They were delicious. My dad and I ate them all."

I was surprised. There had been eight large, over-sized muffins in that box. "Well, come on in and have another one." I stepped back to let her enter. "Do you like coffee?" I asked, not waiting for her to answer before leading the way to the kitchen.

"I love coffee," she said from behind me. "My mother always got mad when I drank it, though. She said it would give me discolored teeth."

I chuckled and glanced over my shoulder. "Well, I suppose if you drink a lot of it, it might, but they have whitening toothpaste for that. Have a seat at the table, and I'll bring it over." She sat down, and I brought the coffee pot and cups, then made another trip for creamer and the muffins. When I returned to the table, Dixie was rubbing up against her leg, and she was scratching his ear, grinning.

"Oh, you've made a friend for life now. Dixie loves people, and he loves scratches."

"He's so cute. I always wanted a cat, but my mother said they shed, and we couldn't have one."

I frowned. "Wait, your mother ran an animal rescue. She didn't even have any pets of her own?" I sat down across from her and poured coffee into both cups.

She looked at me and shook her head. "No, we didn't have any pets. I always wanted a kitten. I begged her for one, but she wouldn't let me have it."

"I'm shocked. Honestly, I thought y'all had to have several animals, at the very least. And cats are very little trouble." The Lynch family was full of surprises.

She nodded as she stirred her coffee. "That's what I told her."

"Katie, can I ask you about the rescue? There's a rumor going around town that your mother was selling rescued animals to a medical lab. Is that true?" I studied her for her reaction.

She looked at me, her face going pale. "Lab? What kind of lab?"

"The kind of lab where they do medical experiments on cats and dogs."

Her eyes went wide, and she shook her head. "No,

that's not true. My mother would never do something like that. Who told you that?"

I shrugged. "It's a rumor going around town. I'm glad to hear that it's not true."

She shook her head again. "No, that never happened. I'm certain of it. Who could do something that awful to a kitten?"

She may have felt certain about it, but there was something in the way she was shocked to hear about it that made me wonder if she knew whether her mother was doing that.

"I feel the same way. Kittens are so adorable I can't imagine anyone doing that to them. Katie, did you have a difficult relationship with your mother?"

She looked up at me, and tears sprang to her eyes. She nodded. "Yes. My mother didn't like me very much. That's why I was surprised when you said that she bragged about me."

My heart broke for her. She seemed immature for her age, and almost innocent, like a child. "It's true that she bragged about you. She was very proud of you. But some people have trouble expressing their feelings."

She pushed her glasses back up on her nose. "I guess."

"I'm sorry she didn't tell you herself how proud she was of you. Sometimes mother-daughter relationships can be complicated."

She smiled lopsidedly. "She was always angry. I could never do anything right."

I poured creamer into my cup. "I'm sorry. I don't know why people are like that sometimes."

She nodded. "Me either. I still miss her, though. I can't believe that she's dead."

"Of course you do. Just because you had a difficult relationship with her doesn't mean that you didn't love her."

Dixie hopped up on his hind legs, placing his front paws on her leg, begging to be petted. She smiled and scratched his ears again. "He's so cute."

"That dixie is a character. I got him from your mother's animal rescue, you know."

She looked up at me. "I don't know what's going to happen to the rescue now that she's gone. She put a lot of effort into it, even if some people think she didn't. I asked my dad what was going to happen to it, but he said he didn't know yet."

"I'm sure it took a lot of time and energy to run the rescue. Katie, what was your mom and dad's relationship like?"

She gazed at me for a few moments before answering. "They fought ever since I was little. They would scream at each other almost every night. I used to lie in my bed and cry, but when I got older, I got some headphones, so I didn't have to listen to it anymore."

My mouth dropped open. I could just imagine the little blonde girl that Katie had been having to listen to that every night. It would warp one's sense of themselves and their sense of how marriage should be. "Katie, I'm so sorry."

She took a deep breath and nodded. "Thank you. I never told anyone before. I never could invite any friends over to my house because I knew they would fight like that, and I didn't want to be embarrassed, so I went to their house for sleepovers."

I shook my head. "There's no excuse for that. They should have gotten counseling, or they should have divorced. A divorce would be better than living like that. Putting you through that was uncalled for." I suddenly felt protective of this young woman.

She took a sip of her coffee. "That was what I came to tell you." She licked her bottom lip and then quickly took another sip of her coffee before continuing.

When she didn't continue, I asked, "Why did you come to see me?" I passed a small plate with a muffin on it to her.

She nodded in thanks. "There's something my dad didn't tell you. And he didn't tell your husband either. Your husband is the detective on the case, isn't he?"

I grabbed a muffin for myself and started peeling the paper liner. "Yes, Alec is my husband."

She nodded. "I thought so. Anyway, he didn't tell you something. A few days before my mother died, he filed for divorce."

I looked at her, my eyes wide. "What? Why wouldn't he mention this? Alec needs to know all the details of what was going on in your mother's life before she was murdered so that he knows what direction to take the investigation."

Tears sprang to her eyes again. "That's what I thought. I told my dad he needed to tell him everything, but he told me to keep my mouth shut. Most of the time, my dad and I get along just fine, but this is important for the detective to know."

I nodded. "It certainly is. How soon before her murder did he file?"

"I don't know the exact date, but I overheard him on the phone telling somebody he had filed but hadn't told my mom. He said she would be served within a few days after he filed, but I don't know if that ever happened."

I was stunned at this. "Your mother never mentioned having received papers?"

She shook her head. "No. She never mentioned it, but she was preoccupied with the fundraiser."

I took a sip of my coffee. "Other than being preoccupied with the fundraiser, did anything seem off with her? Was she upset? Crying?"

She shook her head again. "No, she seemed like her regular self. I have a feeling that she never got the papers served to her. Or maybe she was served at the community center that morning, and whoever served the papers to her killed her." Her eyes met mine now. We stared at one another, each of us thinking our own thoughts for what felt like a long time.

"Who do you think would have served the paperwork?" I asked, breaking the silence.

She shrugged. "I'm not sure how that's done."

I shook my head. "No, I don't think it happened that way. I think either the lawyer's office will serve the paperwork, or maybe the sheriff. But I don't see why whoever served the paperwork would want to kill her. You think your father did it, don't you?"

She took a deep breath, and for a moment, she looked like she had aged twenty years. "Maybe. Their fights were so violent that I'm surprised they didn't kill one another years ago. I don't know why they stayed together all those years, but my father is trying to hide this information, and it makes me wonder."

"You need to talk to Alec and tell him this. He needs to know what's going on." I took a bite of my muffin.

"I don't like talking to the police. I mean, not that I've had much experience with that, but I don't know. It scares me."

"People in authority scare you, don't they?"

She nodded, looking away.

"When a child has been raised in a challenging situation, they sometimes fear authority. But there's nothing to be afraid of. Alec will just want to ask you some questions and find out what you know."

She looked up at me now. "But he'll tell my father. He'll have a fit if he finds out I told."

"Alec will not tell your father, especially if he suspects he murdered your mother. He will keep everything to himself until he investigates and figures out what happened and whether he did murder your mother. Honey, I am so sorry that you are going

through this. I can't imagine how difficult it must be."
I wanted to cry for Katie. She lost her mother, and now she might lose her father, and it might be because she told his secrets. Not to mention what she had lived through as a child.

She nodded again and took a bite of the muffin. There were no tears this time. I grabbed my phone from the kitchen counter and called Alec.

CHAPTER 15

"I'm shocked by what Katie said about her parents, and especially about her father filing for divorce without telling his wife," Lucy said as she made a left into the animal rescue parking lot. "But at least it's not true that Lori was selling dogs and cats to a lab for experiments."

"Me too," I said. "But I'm not sure Katie knew whether her mother was selling them to a lab or not. The look on her face said she was stunned. She really didn't know." I hoped Lori wasn't involved in that, and the more I heard about it, the more I thought it didn't happen. If it had, someone else would have known.

She nodded. "Alec will find out the truth about it,"

she said as she parked, and we got out of the car, heading inside.

"I know he will. I'm glad Katie trusted me enough to come and talk to me."

"Me too. And I am so excited to get that calico kitten," she said.

I grinned. After much cajoling, Lucy had gotten Ed to agree, and I had decided I was going to bring the black one home. Dixie needed a mini-me, didn't he?

We headed inside to a chorus of yipping dogs, and I smiled. I hoped they would all have their forever homes soon.

Anna walked past the desk as we were standing there, and she smiled. "Well, how are you ladies this afternoon? What can I help you with?"

"Hello, Anna," I said. "Lucy and I were here the other day, and we saw two of the most adorable kittens in the back that we would like to adopt."

She grinned. "That's good news. Let's go back and find your kittens."

We followed her through the double doors, and the dogs barked to a mounting crescendo when they saw us. I turned to Anna. "How are things going,

Anna?" I had to raise my voice to be heard over the dogs.

She nodded. Her hair was in a ponytail again, and she wore the same type of khaki uniform top that Gerald had worn when we had been here last. "It's going great. You know, I hate to capitalize on someone's death, but I went to Alan Lynch and told him I would like to take over the rescue. Not just as an employee, but as the owner."

"Oh, that's great news!" Lucy said. "You love the animals so much."

She nodded and grinned again. "He said he thought we could come to some sort of agreement in the coming weeks, but of course, he wasn't in the mood to discuss it just yet with Lori's death and all. Maybe I should have waited a while, but I needed some money to buy supplies for the animals, so I thought I would just bring it up."

"Sounds promising," I said. "I bet you would do a great job running this place and making sure all the animals went to good homes."

She nodded. "You bet I would. I do most of the work anyway, and Lori always took shortcuts. She bought the cheapest food and didn't care one way or another if the animals got enough exercise." She shook her head in disgust.

We walked up to the cages with the cats in them, and I spotted the little black kitten right away. "There he is. Or she. I have no idea if it's a he or she. I didn't even look."

Anna stopped at the cage, unlocked it, and picked up the black kitten. "You're a feisty little guy, aren't you?" She handed him over to me. "He's a boy."

"Oh, he is so sweet," Lucy said, scratching his ear.

I kissed the top of his head. "He's going to be so much fun. It's been years since we had a kitten in the house. I just hope Dixie likes him as much as I do."

Anna closed the cage to keep the other three kittens in and stepped back. "Lucy, where is that calico? Is it that one?" She pointed to a cage with a dark-colored calico in it, but that one was larger than the one we had seen previously.

Lucy shook her head. "No, that's not her. She was in this cage over here." She pointed out the cage, but it was empty.

Anna frowned. "Somebody came in and adopted her yesterday morning. I'm sorry."

"Oh," Lucy said, drawing the word out. "That's

awful. I knew I should have come back sooner to get her."

"There are lots of other cats," I said. "Do you see another one you like? You were looking at a Siamese the other day."

"The Siamese went with the calico," Anna said. "But we've got thirty other cats here."

Lucy looked over the cages, but I could tell by the look on her face she had her heart set on that calico, and none of these were going to do.

"I don't know," she said. "They're all adorable, but I really wanted that calico."

"Maybe if you hold some of them," I said as the kitten in my arms slapped at my hair. "I bet one will appeal to you."

She nodded. "I suppose. Look at that white one back there." She pointed at a small white kitten in the back of a cage.

Anna opened it, picked the kitten up, and handed it to her. "That's a girl."

Lucy scratched her ear, and the kitten meowed.

"That might be your cat," I said.

Lucy chuckled and held the kitten close. "Just give me a minute or two to bond."

I nodded and turned to Anna. "The animals seem to like Gerald."

She nodded. "Yeah, Gerald's been here as long as I have. He's kind of a grumpy guy, but he does a good job. He makes sure things are taken care of. Lori never gave him the respect he deserved. She thought he was disgusting because he was always dirty. I pointed out to her he was dirty because he was doing all the dirty work around here, but it didn't faze her. All she could see was the outside."

"She was a hard person to work for, wasn't she?" I asked.

She nodded. "She was the worst. I don't have respect for a woman who runs a rescue like this and then isn't involved every day. She was awful to the volunteers, and that's why we never seem to have enough of them. I told her she should spring for a pizza now and then to keep them happy, but she wouldn't do it. She said she wasn't going to waste her money on them."

"Are you serious? That's the least she should have been doing for them," Lucy said as the kitten nuzzled her.

She nodded. "That was Lori. I know I should feel bad because she was murdered, but I don't. She was an awful person, and I'm pretty sure she was pocketing some of the donations that were coming in. Otherwise, this place would have been updated years ago, and the animals would be eating better food. I personally know many people who donate a lot of money."

"I imagine it would be expensive to run this place. The basic needs alone would be high," Lucy pointed out.

She sighed. "Yeah, it's expensive. But I'm telling you, she had some big donors. People who have nothing better to do with their money than to throw it at this place."

"Anna, I need to ask you about a rumor I heard going around town. Was Lori selling dogs and cats to a lab in Vermont? A lab that did medical experiments on them?"

Anna's eyes widened. "What? What are you talking about?"

"It's a rumor I heard. Please tell me it isn't true," I said.

She shook her head. "No, it's not true. I can see where people might think she was doing something like that because, honestly, it sounds like something she would do. But she didn't. I arranged most of the rescues and I checked out every organization that was going to take any animals from us. Thoroughly. I would not let any group that looked sketchy come anywhere near these animals. No way."

"Oh, what a relief," Lucy said. "It would have been horrible if that were true."

I was relieved as well. "I'm so glad you do such a thorough job checking into the organizations that are looking for rescue animals. I was so worried when I heard about that."

She nodded. "That will never happen on my watch."

As I gazed at Anna, I hoped that Alan would sell her the rescue. Anna clearly loved the animals, and she would do right by them.

"Has your husband found her killer yet?" she asked, leaning on the cages.

I shook my head. "Not yet, but hopefully soon."

She nodded. "Lori had no business running this rescue because she was an awful human being. Gerald knew how much she looked down on him, and he hated her. I told him not to let it get to him, but it's hard not to let something like that bother you, you know?"

I nodded. "I understand. So, he really couldn't stand her?"

"Oh yeah, he threatened to quit all the time, and then he told me that if he could get his nerve up, he would shut her mouth permanently." She chuckled. "Don't go thinking he was serious about it because he wasn't. Gerald can get pretty grumpy, and she agitated him. Maybe we're awful people, but we haven't shed a tear over her death, and we never will." She turned to Lucy. "What do you think, Lucy? Is that your kitten?"

Lucy smiled. "I don't think I can leave this little sweetie behind."

"That's what I wanna hear," Anna said. "Let's go into the office and fill out the adoption paperwork."

I grinned as we walked back to the office. We were both adopting kittens today. Life didn't get much better than that.

CHAPTER 16

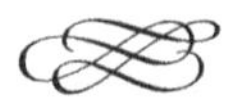

Unfortunately, Dixie and the new kitten weren't immediately bonding, so I was trying to keep them separate when I wasn't around. After locking the kitten in the bathroom before leaving the house, I dropped by Alec's office the following day to take him to lunch, but I had ulterior motives as well. I was on pins and needles, waiting to find out what Alan Lynch had told him about filing for divorce shortly before Lori died and then failing to mention it to him.

I leaned over his desk and kissed him. "Are you hungry? Because I am starved. Where do you want to go for lunch?"

He shrugged and stood up. "I don't have a preference. You choose."

"Seafood?"

He chuckled. "You know I'm a sucker for good seafood." We headed out the door, and he locked it behind him. We said hello to a few people as we exited, and when we got outside, I grabbed his hand and looked up at him.

"So, don't keep it a secret. What happened with Alan Lynch?"

He rolled his eyes and shook his head. "I'd love to know. I can't get a hold of him. I've called his cell phone, but it goes directly to voicemail. I left a message with his secretary to have him call me back immediately, but I haven't heard a thing. I'm going to go down to his office and make him make time for me after lunch."

"I bet he knows what you're going to talk to him about, and he's trying to avoid you."

"I think so, too. I can't get over the fact that he conveniently left that bit of important information out when I interviewed him."

I snorted, disgusted with the whole thing. "We both know it wasn't an accident that he didn't tell you. Did he really think no one was going to find out?

I bet one of the lawyers in his firm is handling the divorce, and he knew they would keep it quiet."

He nodded as we got to his car. "It wouldn't surprise me. He may have canceled the divorce after she was murdered."

"You mean after he murdered her," I said.

"Detective Blanchard!" We looked to see who was calling him and I was surprised to see it was Alan. He hurried across the parking lot, smiling and shaking his head. "Hey, Detective. I'm so sorry I didn't get back to you sooner. I've been in a meeting all morning, and that's why my phone was shut off. When I was getting ready to leave for lunch, my secretary told me you had called, so I thought I would just stop by. Please tell me you found my wife's killer."

Alec studied him for a few moments before answering. "No, I haven't found your wife's killer yet. But I have some questions for you."

Alan looked perplexed now. "Oh? What kind of questions?" He glanced at me.

Alec leaned against his car. "It has come to my attention that you filed for divorce from your wife shortly before she was murdered, and you forgot to tell me about that. How is it possible you didn't tell me?"

Alan's eyes widened. "Yeah, I filed for divorce. Honestly, once I found out about Lori being murdered, I guess I just didn't even think about it." He glanced at me again. "Allie, how are you doing?"

I smiled. Changing the subject wasn't going to work this time. "I'm good."

He nodded and turned back to Alec. "I'm so sorry. I guess that would have been important information to have."

Alec studied him again, playing it cool. "It's very important information to have. It would have changed the entire trajectory of my investigation."

His brow furrowed. "What are you saying? You're not saying that you would have had your eye on me, are you?" He looked at me helplessly.

"What do you think?" Alec said. "A woman is found murdered, and her husband has just filed for divorce? And maybe he didn't even tell his wife he was going to do it?"

The blood drained from Alan's face. "Oh no, wait a minute. I didn't have anything to do with my wife's death. Sure, we had our problems. Well, obviously we had problems because we were going to get a divorce. But I didn't want to murder her, and I *didn't* murder her."

"Is it true that you didn't tell her about the divorce before you filed?" I asked. I should have kept my mouth shut, but that was something I had never been good at.

He sighed. "Okay, yeah, it's true. I filed for divorce without telling Lori first. Not that I didn't want to tell her, but you have to understand that she was an angry woman. She would smile for everybody else, but when it came to me and Katie, she was always angry. We fought a lot, and I didn't want to start something. She had that fundraiser she was working on, and I knew if she knew about the divorce, she would have a fit. I figured it was safer to keep it to myself for as long as I could."

"Why didn't you just wait until after the fundraiser if you were so worried about it?" I asked. "You could have told her then."

"You didn't know Lori. Not the real Lori. I figured she was so busy with the fundraiser that she wouldn't have time to check up on me. That would give me a few extra days to get things packed and out of the house before she even noticed. Believe me, it was safer that way. Katie was at college, so she could avoid Lori's wrath, and I had rented an apartment in Bangor. It was the perfect time for me to file for divorce. She was going to be served the morning of the fundraiser, and I would be out of town when she got it."

That explained why he wasn't there helping her at the community center.

"Who served her the paperwork?" Alec asked. "And at what time was it served?"

"My lawyer served it. Danica Blevins. She told me she served it at 7:00 in the morning."

"Did everything look okay to her when she went in there? Was Lori behaving normally? And what happened when she gave her the paperwork?" Alec asked. I could see some of the anger dissipating from his face.

"She said everything was fine until, of course, she handed her the paperwork and had her sign for it. That was when Lori got angry and started screaming at her. Danica didn't explain to her what was in the envelope, but I'm sure Lori knew who she was. Danica got the signature and left with Lori following her out the door, screaming. She left her there in the parking lot, and that was the last time she saw her."

Alec took all of this in. "So the killer was in and out that morning," he said, glancing at me. "You and

Lucy showed up just before eight o'clock. That didn't give the killer much time to kill her."

"That explains why rigor mortis hadn't set in," I said. "She had just been murdered before we got there." I shivered, wondering if the killer had still been in the building when we got there. My knocking on all the doors may have saved us by scaring them off. I turned to Alan. "That really stinks, finding out that your husband is divorcing you without telling you in advance and then dying minutes later."

He nodded, looking away. "Yeah, I never in a million years would have thought that was what was going to happen. Her last minutes were spent fuming at me. I had shut off my phone and was packing my things. Honestly, I thought she might come back to the house and attack me. She might have done it too if the killer hadn't stepped in."

"If that's what happened, why didn't you tell me?" Alec asked.

"Because I figured you would accuse me. Honestly, when you came to the door to tell me that Lori was dead, I thought for sure you would. No way could I tell you I had just had her served with divorce papers, especially since I hadn't told her before filing. I guess there's something a little low about that, isn't there?

But I couldn't stay with her any longer. It wasn't good for either of us. Poor Katie has suffered the most throughout our marriage, and I wish I had had the courage to leave her years ago. I had nothing to do with my wife's death. I would never have wished that on her, not for anything. You have to believe me."

He had just gone from forgetting he had filed for divorce to admitting he withheld that information. I hated to admit it, but I believed him that he didn't kill her. Hopefully, I wasn't mistaken.

Alec nodded. "I don't want you leaving the area without notifying me. If there's anything else that you have neglected to tell me about your wife or this case, you're going to jail."

He shook his head. "I swear there's nothing else. I just want you to find my wife's killer. Katie deserves to know that her mother has received justice. And I want that for Lori, too."

"We'll be in touch." Alec nodded at me, and we got into the car. Alan turned and went back to his car.

Alec started the car and looked at me. "I just don't know. I kind of feel like he was telling us the truth, but I believed he was the grieving husband, too." He pulled out of the parking space. "I'll have to keep my eye on him."

CHAPTER 17

"How is Dixie doing with the new kitten? And what did you name him?"

I glanced at Lucy as we ran down the street in a middle-class neighborhood not far from her house.

I shook my head. "Not so well. Dixie is livid that a little stranger has encroached on his domain. And I still haven't named him. What about your kitten? How is she doing, and how is Ed adjusting to her? Please tell me he's not growling and hissing at her like Dixie is doing to our kitten."

She laughed. "He's done a little growling, if you want to know the truth. But I've also caught him snuggling with her in front of the television. She is happy as a clam, but she's a little feisty. She likes to grab my feet when I walk past her."

"That's cute," I said, breathing in deeply as we ran along at a slow pace. It was a beautiful day, and the sun was shining. "What did you name her?"

"I am debating on Snowball or Princess."

I chuckled. "Both names are lovely. She's going to be so spoiled."

"I bought her a pink collar with diamonds around it. Well, not real diamonds, but you know what I mean. There's a little bell that jingles when she walks, and she is the prettiest little thing."

"I've got to come by and see her in her new collar. I bet she's just gorgeous. I wish Dixie would get along with our new baby, but I'm worried about him a little. When Alec and I aren't home, I put the kitten in the bathroom and close the door so that Dixie doesn't hurt him."

She glanced at me. "Do you think he would?"

"I don't know for sure, and I hate thinking that he might, so that's why I'm locking him in the bathroom just to be sure. Maybe he'll settle down in time and accept the new kitten." I had to admit that I was a little worried about whether Dixie was ever going to accept the kitten. But it had only been two days, so we needed to give him some time.

We ran along in silence for a few more minutes when I spotted a familiar-looking figure up ahead. I nudged Lucy and nodded in that direction.

"Is that Gerald?" she said breathlessly.

"Yes, I'm pretty sure it is." As we watched, he opened the lid of a trash bin and tossed in an animal carrier. We both gasped and looked at one another.

"What do you suppose he's doing?" she asked.

I shook my head. "I don't know, but that carrier seemed a little heavy when it went in."

"You don't think there was something in it?"

"I don't know, but let's go see." I couldn't imagine why there would be anything in the carrier or why he was even tossing it out. From where we were, it looked like it was in good condition.

"I hope it's empty," she said.

"Gerald!" I called.

Having heard his name, Gerald looked in the opposite direction.

"Gerald!" I called again.

He turned this time and looked in our direction, staring at us as if he didn't recognize us.

When we got closer, I smiled at him. "Gerald, how are you doing?"

He realized then who we were and gave us a bit of a smile. "Oh, hello. How are you ladies doing? And how are the kittens that you adopted? Anna told me you came back."

"My little baby is doing great," Lucy said, still out of breath.

"My little guy is doing well too, although my older cat, Dixie, is not at all pleased to have a little brother," I said.

He nodded. "It sometimes takes older cats a little time to get used to a new one. Especially since kittens can be full of spunk and like to torment the older cats. I bet if you give it a little time, they'll get along just fine."

I nodded. "Yes, I'm sure they'll get things sorted out. I just hope it will be soon. I'm having to separate them when I'm not at the house. I worry too much that Dixie will hurt the baby."

"That's a good idea," he said. He glanced down the street, then turned back. "How is your husband doing with the investigation into Lori's death?"

I took a deep breath. "He's still working on it. He's

hoping to have answers soon. I still can't imagine who would want to kill her."

He grimaced. "I can think of a long list of people who would want to kill her. Honestly, she wasn't a nice person."

"Just because somebody doesn't like someone doesn't mean they would kill them," Lucy pointed out. "Do you know anyone who would genuinely kill someone? I think it takes a lot to commit a crime like that."

He stuck his hands into the pockets of his jeans. "Yeah, I suppose. I guess it's just a mystery who killed her."

"Gerald, when I mentioned the rumor going around town that Lori was selling animals to that lab in Vermont, you didn't tell me whether that was true. Is it?" I asked. Anna had said it wasn't happening, but I wanted confirmation.

He shook his head. "No, it's not true. I was just shocked that a rumor like that was going around town, and that's why I didn't answer. It wasn't until later that I realized I didn't even tell you it wasn't true. I don't know why people have to make up things like that and spread them around like they're the truth. Lori was an awful person, but not even she was that awful."

I nodded, glancing at the trash bin. We had just seen him toss a carrier in. Was there something in it? An animal? Maybe Gerald was the one who was selling animals to the lab. Maybe he and Lori had argued over him doing that, and he had killed her for it.

"We just noticed you throwing a pet carrier into that trash bin," I said, nodding toward it. "It looked like there was something in it."

His brow furrowed, and then he realized what I was saying. "What? Have you lost your mind? Do you think I would throw away a pet carrier with an animal in it?"

I shrugged. "It looked like it was heavy. Was there anything in it?"

"It also looked like it was a new pet carrier," Lucy pointed out. "Why would you throw away a new pet carrier?"

He rolled his eyes. "I didn't throw away a new pet carrier. It's at least six months old, and I wouldn't have thrown it away, but the handle on it cracked and it can't be fixed. You can't carry around a pet carrier without a handle. Or at least you can't do it without it being awkward."

"Can we see it?" I asked, knowing I was pushing him. He was a persnickety person, and I might have been pushing him too far.

He scowled. "Sure, there's the trash bin. Go look."

Lucy and I glanced at each other, and then we went over to the bin and opened the lid. Sure enough, the pet carrier didn't appear to have much wear on it, but the handle was missing. Lucy tilted the carrier so we could see inside of it, and it was empty.

"Satisfied?" Gerald said. "I swear, people around here have lost their minds. First, they think we're selling animals to a lab, and now they think I'm throwing pets into the trash bin. What's the matter with you two?"

Lucy dropped the lid, closing the trash bin. "You never can tell," she said to him. "We just don't want any animals to be harmed."

He rolled his eyes. "Neither do I! That's why I work at the animal rescue. I want to help animals find good homes. As for who killed Lori? I don't have a clue. I wish I did because I would shake their hand."

"Why do you dislike her so much?" I asked. It

seemed like even though she may have been a terrible boss, Gerald disliked her more than was warranted.

He shook his head and muttered something I couldn't make out. Then he said, "I don't have any respect for her at all. She should have been down at the animal rescue doing the hard, dirty work that Anna and I do. I've got things to do. You get out of here now." He turned and headed back to his house.

Lucy and I broke into a trot, continuing our run down the street. When we were out of earshot, I turned to her. "He's cranky."

"Yeah, and he really couldn't stand Lori. It makes me wonder."

It made me wonder, too.

CHAPTER 18

After our run, we dropped by the Cup and Bean coffee shop to see if Mr. Winters had found out anything new. He was sitting at his usual corner table with Sadie beneath it, enjoying a pup cup. We grabbed a coffee and a scone and headed over.

"Good morning, Mr. Winters," I said, sitting across from him. Lucy sat next to me.

He looked up from his newspaper. "Good morning, ladies. It's a beautiful day, but I hear it's going to be warm."

I nodded. "It feels like it's going to get warm later today. Mr. Winters, have you found out anything new about the murder?" I glanced around to make sure no one was close enough to hear what I had said, but everyone seemed to be absorbed in their own conversations.

"The only thing I found out was that Diana Lane is a liar. No one else I've talked to has heard about the animal rescue selling animals to a lab. Then I found out from Cheryl Johnston that Diana couldn't stand Lori because she wouldn't allow her to adopt a dog last year."

"Why wouldn't she allow her to adopt a dog?" Lucy asked. "That was the business she was in."

"Apparently, Lori thought Diana was animal hoarding. She had already adopted six animals from the rescue the prior year. When she came in for that seventh one, Lori turned her down and she got angry." He looked at me over the edge of his cup of coffee.

I stared at him. "So, you're telling me that Diana was just bad-mouthing Lori because she didn't like her?"

He shrugged. "It sounds like it to me. But I only talked to a dozen people, so maybe the people I spoke to just weren't aware of the rumors. Has Alec found out anything about it?"

"He's been doing some investigating, and there's

no indication of it happening." I took a bite of my strawberry scone.

"That's good news," Lucy said, and took a sip of her coffee.

Mr. Winters nodded. "That is good news. Unfortunately, I haven't found out anything new about the murder. Everybody seems shocked that it happened, with about half of the people saying she deserved it and the other half saying she was a saint." He rolled his eyes. "What are you gonna do? People are going to believe what they want to believe."

"That's interesting," I said. "I guess the people who think she was a good person were people she treated well."

He nodded. "Ayup."

"Mr. Winters, we adopted kittens," Lucy announced. She was beaming when she said it.

Mr. Winters grinned. "That's great news. Life is better with a little furry friend, isn't it?"

I reached beneath the table and patted Sadie on the head. "Sure is. But Dixie is having a hard time adjusting to the kitten I adopted. He's all black, just like Dixie, so maybe he's just jealous."

"You should have gotten an orange cat," Lucy said. "Then you would have Halloween covered."

I looked at her with one eyebrow raised. "That is a great idea. Why didn't you think of it earlier and tell me?"

She shrugged. "I'm not perfect."

I chuckled and took a sip of my coffee.

I glanced up at the counter and saw Jeremy Winthrop placing an order. I nudged Lucy and nodded in his direction.

"I still wonder about him," she whispered.

I nodded. "Me too."

When Jeremy got his drink and his muffin, he went and sat at a table across the room.

"I'll be back in a minute," I said, picking up my cup of coffee and heading over to where he was sitting.

"Good morning, Jeremy," I said when I got to him.

He looked up, surprised to see me. "Well, hello, Allie. How are you doing this morning?"

I nodded. "I'm doing great. My friend Lucy and I adopted kittens from Lori's animal rescue. We wanted to do something in her memory." That was a lie, but it would serve my purposes.

"Well, that's really sweet of you. I like cats, but my dog doesn't." He chuckled.

I smiled. "Your dog has no taste."

He chuckled and took a sip of his coffee. "I tell her

that all the time. How is the investigation going? Has your husband mentioned it lately?"

If only he knew it was almost the only thing we talked about. "Oh yes, he's mentioned it. I'm certain he's going to find the killer very soon. I'd hate to be in their shoes. They'll spend the rest of their lives in prison." I watched his face for his reaction to my words. His eyes widened slightly, and he looked away for a moment. When he returned his gaze to me, he seemed composed again.

"I sure hope he can make an arrest soon."

"Jeremy, you and Lori were having an affair, weren't you?" I hated to be so blunt, but it was all over town, anyway.

He closed his eyes for a moment, and when he looked back up at me, he nodded. "Yes, we were having an affair. I didn't know what I was getting into when it began."

"What does that mean?" I asked.

"Lori was something else. She could be sweet when she wanted to be, or she could be mean. She wanted to control absolutely everything in her life. I don't know why she was like that, but I have the feeling that her childhood was out of control. Her parents were alcoholics and would leave her alone for days on end. I just think that made her feel insecure."

Hearing this made me feel sad for Lori. "I can imagine how that would make a child feel insecure."

"Yes, and she felt the need to control everything around her because of it, including me. I can only imagine how things were going at her house with her husband and daughter. Especially her daughter. She would complain about her all the time. Poor Katie just didn't measure up."

"Really? She always told me she was proud of her daughter. I would run into her here at the coffee shop, the grocery store, or someplace else around town, and she would tell me all the things that Katie was achieving."

His eyes met mine. "It wasn't true. Lori was big into appearances and controlling how people viewed those appearances. She wanted everybody to think that she was proud of her daughter because she was achieving so much, but Katie could never achieve enough to make Lori happy."

I shook my head. "That's one of the saddest things I've ever heard. That poor girl is so sweet, and she didn't deserve that."

"No, she didn't deserve that. I tried to get away from Lori, but she threatened to tell people we were having an affair. I was married when it first began, and she said she would tell my wife. But even after I got divorced over some other issues, she threatened to badmouth me around town. I should have told her I didn't care, but there was something about her that made me know she would stop at nothing to destroy me and my career, if it was possible."

"That's terrible."

He nodded. "She didn't like anybody, and she didn't approve of what anyone was doing. Even though her animal rescue was successful, she wasn't happy about that either. She was going to fire Gerald and Anna, you know. I told her she would be crazy to fire them, especially Anna because they were essentially running the place. They cared for those animals, and they would do anything for them."

"She was going to fire them? What was her reasoning?" I asked and took a sip of my coffee.

"She felt like they could have done a better job keeping the place clean, finding people to adopt the animals, or finding other rescues to send them to. But there's only so much one person can do, right? Or rather, two. But she hated Anna. Anna stood up to her, and she didn't like that one bit."

"She thought she was better than Anna, right?"

He chuckled. "She thought she was better than everyone. But she was particularly ugly to Anna. Anna baked a coconut cake that looked absolutely delicious for her fundraiser, and she pitched it into the trash." He shook his head. "I couldn't believe it. I was thinking about bidding on it myself."

"Did Anna know she threw it in the trash?"

He shook his head. "No, she wasn't there. I had stopped to see her that morning when Lori was getting everything set up, and she pointed out the cake and said there was no way she was going to auction it off because Anna's house was disgusting. I have no idea if Anna's house is disgusting or not, but I'm telling you, the cake looked great."

"I heard she did things like that, but I didn't know if it was true. That's a shame she behaved that way," I said.

He nodded. "That's just how she was."

Lori was a sad person, and while I wanted to feel sorry for her, it was the people in her life who had suffered the most and at her hands.

I studied him for a moment, then took another sip

of my coffee. “Well, Jeremy, it’s been nice talking to you. I’ll see you around.”

“See you around, Allie.” He took a bite of his blueberry muffin.

I turned to head back to Mr. Winters’s table. Jeremy had just placed himself at the scene of the crime.

CHAPTER 19

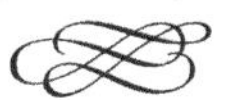

It was hard carrying on a conversation with Lucy and Mr. Winters when everything I knew about Lori Lynch's murder was swirling around my mind. Jeremy had given me another piece of the puzzle, and I couldn't sit at the coffee shop a minute longer. I turned to Lucy. "I've got an errand to run. We need to go." I turned to Mr. Winters. "It's good seeing you again, Mr. Winters, and you too, Sadie," I said, looking under the table at the poodle. She wagged her tail, and I patted her head before standing up.

Lucy got to her feet and grabbed her coffee. "I need to stop by the grocery store and pick up some milk if you don't mind."

I nodded and we headed out to the car.

"Where are we going?" she asked.

"The rescue shelter." I grabbed my phone from my purse and sent Alec a text.

She looked at me curiously, then nodded and started the car.

The rescue shelter only had two cars in the parking lot when we got there. It was just as well because I recognized those cars. When we went inside, no one was at the front desk.

"I bet they're busy in the back," Lucy said. "What have you got in mind? You were texting an awful lot on the way over."

I turned to her. "Let's go see what's going on in the back." I pushed my way through the double doors, and the dogs started barking. There were fewer animals back here today, so they must have found another rescue to take them.

"Wow, most of the kennels are empty," Lucy said.

I nodded, absentmindedly passing the dogs and

looking around the back. There were four older cats in the cages. "It's a good thing we picked up those kittens when we did."

She nodded. "I'll say. Well, hopefully, they all ended up with good homes. What are we doing here?"

I turned to her and smiled. "Catching a killer."

Her eyes widened, and she nodded. "Gotcha. I'm here for it."

Anna came out of the back room and looked surprised to see us. "Oh, good morning, ladies," she said, heading toward us. "How are those kittens doing? I hope they're adjusting well."

I nodded. "The kittens are doing fabulously. I'm so glad we got them when we did. It looks like you've got a shortage of kittens today."

She smiled. "Isn't it wonderful? We adopted out three more kittens after you took those two the other day, and then we got in touch with another rescue who came and picked the rest of them up. We've just got four cats left. I love it when we can adopt them out or send them to another rescue to adopt them out for us."

"You must have quite a network of other rescues in the country to do all that you do," Lucy said.

She nodded. "Yes, I have a listing of over fifty

rescues that I have vetted myself. It seems odd that there are areas of the country where there isn't a big surplus of animals like we have around here. But I'm glad there are, so our local animals can find a home." She stood smiling, her hair back in the ponytail she usually wore.

"I admire you for the work you do," I said. "It's important work, and the fact that you really throw yourself into it is amazing."

She smiled and blushed. "I can't imagine doing it any other way. I have to know that these animals are going to be taken care of. It's a calling, really."

"Did Lori have a calling?" I asked.

Her face clouded over. "No. The only thing important to her was herself."

Lucy shook her head. "That's a shame."

"You do all of this work here, and you still had time to make a three-layer coconut cake for the fundraiser," I said. "You're a regular dynamo. It's a shame the fundraiser never happened. Are you going to do another one? I know Lori used that fundraiser to make a lot of money for the rescue."

She nodded. "I was just thinking about that this morning. We've got to come up with some sort of fundraiser. Maybe we'll plan another spaghetti dinner. It will take us some time to get things together again, so maybe in the next month or two."

"I would love to have seen your coconut cake," Lucy said. "Didn't you say your mother won a ribbon at the county fair with it?"

She nodded. "Oh yes, my mother made the best coconut cakes, and she taught me how to make them. They're absolutely delicious."

"It's funny that your coconut cake disappeared that morning," I said. "You did say that Lori came by and picked it up, and yet it wasn't there at the community center with the other desserts." I watched her closely for her reaction.

Doubt flickered across her face for a moment. "Oh, I'm sure it was there. She picked it up from my house the day before."

I shook my head. "No, we were at the community center for some time, and we took a few moments to admire all the desserts. A triple-layer cake would be a taller cake and would have stood out to us."

She smiled and shrugged. "Well, I don't know what she did with it then. Maybe she forgot it at home. Was there something I could help you ladies with? Were you looking for another kitten? We'll probably have some more in before you know it."

"No, we don't need any more kittens. We're delighted with the two we got, but they're a handful, as you know kittens are. Anna, you said something to us when we talked to you about Lori picking up those desserts herself. You said that if she didn't approve of the donor's home it had been baked in, she would toss the dessert. And your dessert is missing."

Her eyes widened, and she shook her head. "I don't know what you're talking about. She picked up my cake, and I'm certain it was at the community center."

"We're certain that it wasn't," Lucy said.

She hesitated, shifting her weight from one foot to the other. "Is there something else I can help you with? We've got an awful lot to do around here. We wanted to get all the empty kennels and cages cleaned today, so they're ready to go when more animals come in. It takes a lot to keep everything clean."

"Anna, what happened to your coconut cake?" I asked.

She glared. "Why are you obsessed with my coconut cake? I can make another one, and you can buy it to support the shelter if you want to."

"But what happened to the one you made for the fundraiser?" I asked.

Before I knew what was happening, she pulled a small handgun from her pocket and pointed it at us. "Why do you have to be so nosy? Why can't you just leave things alone?"

Lucy gasped. "What are you doing? Put that thing away!"

She shook her head. "I can't do that. You two have stuck your nose into my business, and you're going to pay for that."

I inhaled. "Anna, it doesn't have to happen like this. I'm sure you didn't mean to hurt Lori," I said carefully.

She laughed. "But I did intend to hurt Lori. She was an evil person, and she threw my coconut cake in the trash. I saw it when I stopped by to see how things were going. It was sitting right there. She didn't even try to hide it. That coconut cake was my mother's recipe, and it was the best coconut cake recipe in the world."

I swallowed. "I'm sure it was delicious. Some people have no taste."

Before I knew what was happening, Lucy reached back behind her, picked up a hard plastic pet carrier from the floor, and threw it at Anna. She screamed as the gun dropped to the concrete floor. Thankfully, it didn't go off, and I lunged for it, but Anna was quicker, and she landed on top of me, shoving me away from the gun.

"What's going on out here?" Gerald hollered as he came around the side of the kennels. When he saw Anna and me wrestling for the gun just a couple of feet away from us, his eyes widened. "What is this?"

Lucy had pulled her phone from her pocket and was dialing the police. "Gerald, help us get the gun away from her," she said as the operator picked up the phone. "I need the police at the animal rescue," she said into the phone.

Gerald turned to look at us as we struggled, then he hurried over and picked up the gun, and held it on me. "Get up."

Anna and I looked at him and slowly got to our feet.

"Gerald, please put that gun down," I said. "You don't want to get involved in this." His eyes were hard as he looked at me.

He shook his head and turned to Anna. "Why did you get yourself into a mess like this?"

She went to him and grabbed the gun from him. "I had to do it. I had to. Everything will be fine. We just need to get rid of these two."

I swallowed. We were really in trouble now.

"Put the gun down," a stern voice ordered from behind us. I looked over my shoulder to see Alec standing there with his gun drawn, and I breathed a sigh of relief.

CHAPTER 20

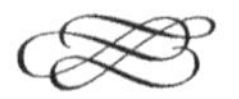

"We brought Snow to visit," Lucy said, sitting down on my couch next to Ed. She opened the pet carrier and let the white kitten out.

"Oh, my goodness, she's grown so much," I said. "And I love her name."

"I couldn't settle on a name, so that's what I came up with," she said.

"Yeah, I told her to name her Cottage Cheese, but she didn't go for it," Ed said, grinning.

Lucy rolled her eyes. "We are not naming her Cottage Cheese."

I chuckled. "It's perfect." I started to say something else when I heard a kitten scream from another room.

"Hold on," I said, jumping up and running to the ballroom where Dixie had cornered the black kitten. "Dixie, stop it!" I scooped up the kitten and brought him back to the living room. "I don't know what I'm going to do about Dixie. He's just awful to this baby."

"I would have thought that he'd have gotten over it by now," Lucy said.

I shook my head. "I've tried everything, and he wants nothing to do with him. I named him Coal, by the way."

"That's a swell name," Ed said.

"I like it," Lucy agreed. "I wish Dixie would lighten up."

I rubbed Coal's head. "Me too."

The front door opened, and Alec appeared in the living room doorway. "Hey. What's going on?" He was home from booking Anna.

"Lucy and Ed brought Snow to visit Coal." I put Coal down next to Snow, and their backs arched, and their hair stood on end, but then they sniffed each other's noses and settled down.

"Look at that. I bet they remember each other from the rescue," Alec said.

I nodded. "I bet they do. They're so sweet together."

He came and sat beside me. "Well, you two are lucky to be alive. It's a good thing you texted me before you headed down there."

I looked at him. "You can say that again."

He sighed. "Don't ever do that again."

I leaned over and kissed him. "Of course not. What did Ana say about murdering Lori?"

He chuckled. "Well, as we all know, Anna hated Lori. She hated her because she didn't take care of the animals properly and because she looked down on her. Anna was good enough to clean litter boxes and kennels but not good enough to be included in any of Lori's parties or get-togethers. When Lori threw her coconut cake into the trash, it was the final straw."

Ed shook his head. "Well, you can't blame her for murdering her. If someone threw my coconut cake in the trash, I might kill them too."

"Especially when it's your mother's coconut cake recipe that won a ribbon at the fair," Lucy agreed. "That takes some nerve."

Alec chuckled. "That seems to make it worse, doesn't it?"

I turned to him. "What did she kill her with? And why was Lori face down on my cake? It hurts my feelings a little bit."

Alec chuckled again. "Anna said she was so stunned when she discovered Lori had thrown her cake in the trash that she couldn't move. Lori sat down at the table to write out another card, and when Anna recovered from the shock, she went around behind her. She carried a short length of steel pipe in her purse and hit Lori in the back of the head with it. Your cake just happened to be the closest one when she fell face forward into it. Anna said she realized what she had done too late."

"What?" I said. "Who carries a length of steel pipe in their purse? Along with that tiny gun she pulled on us?"

"And how could she say it wasn't planned if she was carrying the murder weapon on her?" Lucy asked.

"She said she lives in a dangerous neighborhood, so she keeps a length of pipe in her purse, just in case. But once she had used it, she hid it in her apartment and got the gun for safety. We recovered the pipe, and it's twelve inches in length and heavy enough to kill someone with one blow if you hit them in the right place," he explained.

"Wow." I could think of other weapons to carry besides a piece of pipe.

"She handed over Lori's purse. She had taken it hoping we might think Lori was killed in a robbery," he said. "I'll turn it over to Katie."

"What happened to the coconut cake?" Lucy asked. "If you didn't find it during the investigation, where did it go?"

He smiled. "She grabbed the trash bag that was in the trash can Lori threw the cake in and took it with her so no one would know what she did to it. It embarrassed her. But she forgot to look to see if Lori had already made out a card for her cake."

"All of that had to happen in a short timeframe, didn't it?" Ed asked.

Alec nodded. "There were a lot of people down at the community center that morning. Jeremy was there at about 6:15, Danica Blevins dropped by at around 7:00, then Anna came in right after Danica left, at about 7:10. Anna waited in her car until she left. Then Allie and Lucy got there shortly before 8:00."

"What about the lab rumor?" I asked. "It wasn't true, was it?" Even though Mr. Winters couldn't find anyone to corroborate Diana Lane's story, and others had said it wasn't true, I had to ask.

He shook his head. "It's not true. Yancey help me look into it, and it was just a rumor."

I breathed a sigh of relief. "Thank goodness."

"What about Gerald?" Lucy asked. "He didn't even try to help us. He held the gun on us."

"Did he have something to do with the murder?" I asked. "I bet he did."

He shook his head. "They both said he didn't know anything about it. He heard Anna and you struggling at the rescue and couldn't help but step in to help his friend. He didn't even know what it was about, he just knew he needed to help Anna."

"Oh, it's nice having good friends like that," Lucy said.

I turned and looked at her. "I have a friend like that."

She nodded. "So do I. If you ever get into a mess and are trying to murder someone, I will have your back."

"Thank you, friend. I've got your back, too." I smiled at her. Lucy would be there for me, no matter what.

Alec shook his head. "You two are something else."

"Aren't they, though?" Ed said.

Lucy looked at me. "You never told me how you figured out it was anna who murdered Lori."

I smiled. "When Jeremy Winthrop told me he was at the community center the morning of the murder, I had at first thought that he was placing himself at the crime scene, which he was. But he told me Lori had tossed Anna's coconut cake into the trashcan. I realized that Anna must have dropped by the community center earlier than when we saw her stopping by to decorate after the murder. She knew Lori had thrown her cake away and she was angry about it. I just had a hunch it was her."

"You could have just called me and let me know what you found out *instead* of going down there," Alec pointed out. "It's a good thing you texted me about it and I decided to drop by just in case."

"Yeah, that's what I should have done, but all's well that ends well." I grinned at him.

He sighed and rolled his eyes.

It wasn't until Anna pulled a gun on me that I knew for sure she had killed Lori. The coconut cake was the key.

The kittens were underneath the coffee table, wrestling and having the time of their lives as we talked. "Look at them. I wish Coal and Dixie could get along like that." I looked over and noticed Dixie sitting on the floor near the end of the couch. He was ignoring the kittens, but his tail was swishing. He was angry about the little invaders, and if we hadn't been sitting there, I was sure he would have intervened and stopped their play.

"They're so cute together," Lucy said. "I'll have to bring Snow over regularly so they can visit."

I looked at Dixie again. Anger rolled off his body, even though he was pretending to ignore them. I had gotten him as a kitten, and he had been my only furry love for nine years. Maybe he felt betrayed. The thought broke my heart. "Lucy, maybe you should just take Coal."

She looked at me. "What do you mean, take Coal?"

I sighed. "As much as I want another cat, it's not working out with Dixie. I think he feels slighted by the new kitten. But Coal and Snow obviously love each other, so why don't you take him home and keep him?"

She smiled. "I'd be happy to take him. Are you sure? I know you love him."

I nodded. "I'd rather he be happy, and he would definitely be happier with Snow. And I feel guilty about hurting Dixie's feelings. He's always been number one, and that's the way he should stay."

She smiled. "Then I would be delighted to take him home. It will be so much fun seeing the two of them play. You can come and visit him whenever you want."

I nodded. "You know I will."

I watched the kittens continue their playing under the coffee table. I was a little sad that I wasn't going to get to keep Coal, but I knew it was in the best interest of all three cats if I let him go.

Dixie jumped into my lap, purring. "Look at my handsome boy." I ran my hand along his back, and he closed his eyes in contentment.

Animals enrich our lives in a way that nothing else can, and I was glad Lucy and Ed were going to have the two kittens to do that. Alec reached over and ruffled Dixie's fur. "I've grown attached to this guy."

I nodded. "He's a good boy."

It was a shame that Anna had killed Lori. If she hadn't been guilty of murder, she and Gerald would have done a fantastic job running the animal rescue. They both loved the animals, and they would have made certain they were well taken care of.

The End

SIGN up to receive my newsletter for updates on new releases and sales:

https://www.subscribepage.com/kathleen-suzette

Follow me on Facebook:

https://www.facebook.com/Kathleen-Suzette-Kate-Bell-authors-759206390932120

BOOKS BY KATHLEEN SUZETTE:

A PUMPKIN HOLLOW CANDY STORE MYSTERY

Treats, Tricks, and Trespassing
Gumdrops, Ghosts, and Graveyards
Confections, Clues, and Chocolate

A FRESHLY BAKED COZY MYSTERY SERIES

Apple Pie a la Murder

Trick or Treat and Murder

Thankfully Dead

Candy Cane Killer

Ice Cold Murder

Love is Murder

Strawberry Surprise Killer

Plum Dead

Red, White, and Blue Murder

Mummy Pie Murder

Wedding Bell Blunders

In a Jam

Tarts and Terror

Fall for Murder

A FRESHLY BAKED COZY MYSTERY SERIES

Web of Deceit

Silenced Santa

New Year, New Murder

Murder Supreme

Peach of a Murder

Sweet Tea and Terror

Die for Pie

Gnome for Halloween

Christmas Cake Caper

Valentine Villainy

Cupcakes and Beaches

Cinnamon Roll Secrets

Pumpkin Pie Peril

Dipped in Murder

A Pinch of Homicide

Layered Lies

Cake and Criminals

A COOKIE'S CREAMERY MYSTERY

Ice Cream, You Scream

Murder with a Cherry on top

Murderous 4th of July

Murder at the Shore

Merry Murder

A Scoop of Trouble

Lethal Lemon Sherbet

Berry Deadly Delight

Chilled to the Cone

Sundae Suspects

Stars, Stripes, and Secrets

A LEMON CREEK MYSTERY

Murder at the Ranch

The Art of Murder

Body on the Boat

A Pumpkin Hollow Mystery Series

Candy Coated Murder

Murderously Sweet

Chocolate Covered Murder

Death and Sweets

Sugared Demise

Confectionately Dead

Hard Candy and a Killer

Candy Kisses and a Killer

A LEMON CREEK MYSTERY

Terminal Taffy

Fudgy Fatality

Truffled Murder

Caramel Murder

Peppermint Fudge Killer

Chocolate Heart Killer

Strawberry Creams and Death

Pumpkin Spice Lies

Sweetly Dead

Deadly Valentine

Death and a Peppermint Patty

Sugar, Spice, and Murder

Candy Crushed

Trick or Treat

Frightfully Dead

Candied Murder

Christmas Calamity

A RAINEY DAYE COZY MYSTERY SERIES

Clam Chowder and a Murder
A Short Stack and a Murder
Cherry Pie and a Murder
Barbecue and a Murder
Birthday Cake and a Murder
Hot Cider and a Murder
Roast Turkey and a Murder
Gingerbread and a Murder
Fish Fry and a Murder
Cupcakes and a Murder
Lemon Pie and a Murder
Pasta and a Murder
Chocolate Cake and a Murder

A RAINEY DAYE COZY MYSTERY SERIES

Pumpkin Spice Donuts and a Murder

Christmas Cookies and a Murder

Lollipops and a Murder

Picnic and a Murder

Wedding Cake and a Murder

Made in the USA
Las Vegas, NV
28 June 2024